THE INITIATE

THE INITIATE

BOOK 1

BEN NEIL

Waterside Productions

First Printing, 2025

ISBN-13: 978-1-968401-14-6 print edition
ISBN-13: 978-1-968401-15-3 e-book edition

Waterside Productions
2055 Oxford Ave
Cardiff, CA 92007
www.waterside.com

For Avery,
May all of your dreams come to fruition. You will always
be a part of me.

ACKNOWLEDGMENTS

I believe nothing is ever created without the assistance and support of others. This book came into existence mainly because of the great influence and support I received during the process. I am forever indebted and grateful to all those individuals who helped make this book possible. So many people helped along the way, and without all of them, I might not have completed this project.

I am forever grateful for Sean Fleming. Your encouragement and support were instrumental in the process of writing this book.

I would also like to thank Tyler Tichelaar, my editor, for all of your advice and direction. This book would not be what it is today without your invaluable guidance and support.

I would also like to offer a special thanks to Dr. Greg Reid, for all of your insight and guidance and the introductions you made for me. This book wouldn't be where it is today without you.

Brian Pascal, thank you for believing in me and making the introductions you did. I am forever indebted to you.

Bill Gladstone, my publisher, thanks for believing in me and investing your time and resources into this work. I am eternally grateful for all of your wisdom and guidance. I couldn't have asked for anyone better to help me with this book.

Christopher Van Buuren, thank you for all of your ideas and help with creating a marketing plan for this book.

I'd also like to thank all of the other people who supported me on this journey. I couldn't have done this alone, and I am humbled by the amount of help I received at the times when I needed it most.

Jake Woodhave, thank you for your great friendship and support.

Steve Hall, thank you for your friendship, and for providing me with the encouragement to continue on this path.

So many others who offered me their support on this journey, including Bret Hanna, Brandon Bell, Phil Damon, Ryan Price, Nate Roundy, Byron Goates, Robert Montgomery, Mitchell Milliron, Jasen Penman, Trafton Sayama, Apakorn Leetrakul, Adam Baird, Cameron Coop, Jesse Theurer, Alma Tuck, Tyler Granger, Raphael Cristofoli, John Wallace, John Matkin, David Nielson, Brian Stephens, Trevor Johnson, Mitch Brooks, Jean Russell, Dick Calafato, Denny Malatek, Louise Anderson, Sterling Howell, Marilyn Hin, and anyone else I may have forgotten to mention. Thank you for everything. I couldn't have done this without you.

And lastly to my readers, thank you. My wish is that this book will offer hope and encouragement where it is needed.

PROLOGUE

A million stars glittered like scattered diamonds across the deep velvet sky above the Nile Valley, each one pulsing with an ancient, luminous warmth. It was midsummer, and the full moon had risen high, resting like a polished pearl atop the Great Pyramid, bathing the sands and stone in a ghostly silver glow. Shadows stretched long and slow across the desert floor, cast by palm trees and ancient obelisks, as if time itself had begun to dissolve into the mystic night.

A warm breeze drifted south from the Mediterranean, curling through the valley like a whispered secret. It stirred the silk curtains that framed the royal balcony and carried with it the rich scent of jasmine, the coppery tinge of stone, and the faint electricity of something unseen. Far below, the Nile murmured against its banks, the lapping waters gently stroking the rocks like a lullaby from the Earth itself.

Two figures sat in stillness, silhouetted against the moonlit landscape. One, draped in robes of midnight blue, his dark eyes glowing with centuries of wisdom, was Anubis, hierophant of the Egyptian Mystery Schools. The other, youthful yet cloaked in the stillness of someone far older than his years, was Tutankhamen, boy king and newly risen adept. Between them lay the charged silence of something ending—and something far greater just beginning.

Anubis turned to the boy he had guided for so many years. His voice was low, rich with emotion, and vibrating with a sorrow he did not fully show.

"Tutankhamen," he said, his eyes gleaming with moisture that caught the moonlight, "you must listen to me very carefully. I do not know how much more time we will have together."

Tutankhamen blinked, startled by the gravity in his mentor's voice. He leaned forward, searching Anubis's face for reassurance, but found none.

"What must you tell me that is so urgent it cannot wait until tomorrow?"

Anubis paused. A storm flashed faintly on the far horizon, distant lightning threading through the sky like the fingers of unseen gods. His hand rested gently on the boy's shoulder, grounding him with warmth and the subtle tremor of unspoken knowing.

"I know who you are," Anubis said. "You are not the same soul who entered the lower chamber three weeks ago. From the moment you emerged, I saw it in your eyes. You carry the echoes of another time. A future time. You are not just Tutankhamen. You are a soul returned."

The boy king's breath caught. The words struck him like the hot wind before a sandstorm—unavoidable, powerful, and true. The secret he had carried, heavy and lonely, was no longer his alone.

"Everything you say is true," he confessed, voice unsteady. "But how did you know? Why did you wait to speak of it?"

Anubis leaned in, his voice a reverent hush. "Because you needed time to remember. This is not the first life we have shared. You and I have journeyed together across lifetimes, always seeking, always finding one another again. And this is merely the beginning of your return. You came back to this moment in time to remember who you are, to retrieve a piece of your power."

The storm crept closer. The air thickened. Thunder rumbled low in the sky, vibrating through the stone beneath their feet.

Tutankhamen's body softened, the tension slipping from his shoulders. A quiet strength began to rise in him as he gazed at Anubis, not just as a boy looking at a teacher, but as an ancient companion recognizing an eternal bond.

"Tell me," he said. "Tell me everything you know of what is to come."

Anubis smiled, pride and sorrow etched into the lines of his face. "I will tell you what I can. Soon, the world will change. The Earth itself will shift, and humanity will be brought to its knees. This is the Great Shift of the Ages. The time when mankind must awaken or fall. Our powers—the abilities we have nurtured across countless lives—will be needed. We have been preparing for this. All of us. The initiates. The travelers. The awakened."

Tutankhamen sat straighter now, the flicker of purpose igniting in his chest.

"Will we meet again? How will I find you?"

Anubis looked out across the Nile, where the storm rolled silently over the horizon like a divine procession.

"You will find me the way you always have," he said. "Not through logic or maps, but through the quiet voice within you. Listen to your heart. Follow its rhythm. I will be waiting. And when you come, I may need your help to remember. Will you promise me that?"

The boy hesitated, only for a moment. Then he placed his hand over his chest, where a deep and ancient truth stirred.

"I promise," he said.

And in the sacred hush that followed, the winds shifted once more, carrying their vow into the cosmos—a seed planted in time, waiting to bloom again when the stars were right and the world was ready.

1

The sprawling terminal of London's Heathrow International Airport pulsed with life—a kinetic sea of bodies, voices, and restless energy. Tired eyes scanned glowing departure boards. Children clutched tattered stuffed animals. The scent of jet fuel lingered faintly beneath the stronger aroma of roasted coffee beans and fast food. People moved with anxious purpose, consumed by their private concerns—missed connections, ticking clocks, business deals, reunions, and goodbyes.

Amid this orchestrated chaos, very few had any inkling of the cataclysmic events poised to ripple across the surface of their tidy realities. No one paused to consider how small their worries might seem when viewed from eternity's summit. Their lives felt urgent, important. The men in tailored suits clutched their carry-ons like life-lines, their minds rehearsing the elation they'd feel when promotions were secured and colossal deals closed. They imagined the glow of success like warm sunlight breaking over a mountain range, certain that their arrival at the next meeting would mark a turning point.

All the while, thousands rushed along the terminal's arteries, their collective anxiety forming an invisible fog that hung thick in the air. Each person carried a private burden or silent anticipation, unaware that they might be hours from events that would shatter or awaken them forever.

I sat tucked in the far corner of a cramped coffee shop, a dim oasis of quiet amid the storm. Across the small table sat a man I had only recently come to know—William Allbright. The world outside our booth seemed to vanish as we delved deep into conversation. We were discussing miracles—strange, uncanny alignments that had drawn us together from opposite ends of the globe. I was so absorbed in recounting my time in Egypt, my voice lowered and reverent, that I nearly missed my connecting flight home to Salt Lake City.

William was a man hollowed by tragedy. The well-tailored exterior—his silvered hair, dignified posture, could not conceal the devastation that clung to him like ash. He had lost his wife and only son in a plane crash. Since that terrible day, he had wandered like a ghost through his own life, the meaning that once gave it color now leached away.

Our paths had first crossed in Cairo International Airport—an accidental meeting, or so it had seemed at the time. But there had been something in the way our eyes met, a mutual recognition that bypassed logic. He later told me that from the moment he saw me, he felt drawn to something in my energy, as if I carried a flicker of peace he desperately needed.

And, in truth, I understood. In Egypt, I had encountered a wise man—a figure out of time and myth—who seemed to embody the same serenity William sensed in me. That man had told me that subtle changes would ripple through my life upon my return, and William, in his suffering, seemed to be one of those signs.

I recognized William's pain because I had lived it. Five years earlier, I had lost my wife and daughter in a violent car crash that shattered everything I knew. I shared this tragedy with him, and as I spoke, I looked into his eyes with a kind of fierce compassion. I didn't pretend I could fix him. I didn't promise to carry his pain away. But I hoped my story might offer him a bridge—a way to believe healing was possible.

William listened in stunned silence, his eyes brimming. As I spoke, he clutched his coffee cup tightly, as though it might anchor him. I told him how, in the aftermath of my loss, I had descended into a mental war zone. My mind, once a place of logic and optimism, became hostile territory. Voices whispered all day and all night, reminding me of every failure, every misstep. They accused, tormented, and shredded my remaining will to live.

I watched as recognition flickered across William's face. He knew this battlefield. He was living it.

I explained that these voices had grown so relentless that I had come close—many times—to ending it all. But some sliver of instinct, some desperate ember of hope, drove me to seek answers. I began studying obsessively. I read books on psychology, devoured volumes on Eastern philosophy and ancient wisdom traditions. I began to meditate, not with calm, but with desperation. Slowly, painfully, I learned to hear another voice within me—a quiet, wise one. And with time, I'd aligned myself with it.

As I told William this, doubt clouded his face. I could see the wall go up in his eyes. Perhaps he thought I was deluded or offering spiritual clichés. Maybe he couldn't imagine peace was possible for him.

So I didn't preach. I told him the truth: It had been agonizing. I had wept until my body shook. I had shouted into pillows and begged the Universe for answers. Surrender had not been a gentle release, but a tearing away of the false identity I had so carefully constructed.

"I was no longer John Fullman, the entrepreneur," I said. "No longer husband, no longer father, no longer anything. And that loss forced me to ask, over and over again: Who am I?"

William flinched, and tears began to slide silently down his cheeks.

"I had to let it all go," I continued. "Everything I thought I was. And once I did, I began to feel something else—a connection to something deeper. Something that had been there all along."

I explained that peace didn't arrive as a sudden miracle. It came as moments. Moments of stillness. Of clarity. And eventually, it led to a path I hadn't known existed. The wise ones had called it personal mastery. Their examples—from ancient sages to modern mystics—became my guides. They had suffered, too. They had struggled. But they had also triumphed.

When I told William about my journey in Egypt—the discovery of a code, a connection to the ancient mystery schools—his eyes widened. Hope, faint but real, began to return.

"Tell me more," he whispered. "Tell me about Egypt."

And in that moment, I knew he had taken the first step. His heart, cracked open by loss, was ready to receive something sacred. A light that, once ignited, could never be extinguished.

2

The afternoon sun scorched the Egyptian desert, its blazing rays bearing down with merciless intensity on the gathered crowd outside the Great Pyramid. The air shimmered with heat, turning the horizon into a wavering mirage of gold and dust. Among the crowd, a striking assembly of nobles and holy men stood out, wrapped in vibrant silks of scarlet, sapphire, and emerald. Their robes billowed slightly in the dry breeze, and their gold-inlaid jewelry glinted brilliantly, flashing like fireflies against the endless sweep of sandstone.

At the forefront, Tutankhamen and his queen, Ankhesenpaaten, followed the solemn procession led by Anubis—the imposing hierophant cloaked in jet-black linen—and twelve priests robed in white and gold. Together, they moved toward the yawning maw of the pyramid's entrance, where shadows spilled out like ink from the mysteries within.

As they passed through the ancient threshold, prismatic beams of light refracted from the gemstones that adorned the ceremonial garb of the procession. Rubies, sapphires, emeralds, and diamonds—each one cast brilliant streaks across the stone, as if the very air were alight with divine approval.

Behind them, a somber audience looked on, hearts heavy with the weight of what was to come. Murmurs stilled as Tutankhamen paused with Ankhesenpaaten. They held each other tightly, his youthful arms wrapped around her slender waist. Their eyes met in silent communion, speaking volumes beyond words—of love, of fear, and of the terrible uncertainty that lay ahead.

The pharaoh, though just nineteen, carried the gravitas of many lifetimes. His face, usually serene, bore now the shadow of dread. Ankhesenpaaten, radiant and resolute, pressed her cheek to his chest, tears glistening on her lashes.

"May the gods bless and favor you in this hour," she whispered into his ear, her voice trembling yet strong. "I have seen this moment in my dreams. Do not fear. You shall emerge reborn, free of all that burdens you."

A flicker of calm passed over Tutankhamen. He drew back slightly to look into her eyes. The heat of the desert was nothing compared to the warmth of her touch. "I am not afraid, my dear," he said, voice steady. "I have been walking toward this moment across the sands of many lives. I am ready. In three days, we will see each other again."

She nodded, though sorrow clung to her like the fine dust of the desert. "Three days will feel like an eternity. I will miss your embrace most of all. If only the sands of time could be hastened."

They kissed once more, a tender and lingering farewell, before he turned to follow Anubis and the priests into the bowels of the pyramid. The temperature dropped as they descended, cool shadows swallowing the sweltering light of the world above. The sandstone corridor narrowed with each step, the air thick with the scent of ancient dust and ceremonial myrrh.

As they progressed, the walls grew darker, more primitive—scraped rather than carved—until they reached a narrow stone staircase descending into near-total blackness. Mysterious luminescent stones glowed faintly along the walls, their eerie green and blue lights casting ghostly shadows.

At last, the path opened into the lower chamber—The Pit. Unlike the rough-hewn sandstone above, the chamber was sheathed in polished black granite, every surface reflecting the dim light with a surreal shimmer. In the chamber's center stood a sarcophagus of the same stone, its surface etched with ancient glyphs pulsing faintly with power. Beside it, resting against the wall, loomed its heavy granite lid.

Near the far wall, a wooden table held sacred tools: ritual blades, vials of oil and water, and at the center, resting as if enthroned, was a golden mask—a masterwork of divine artistry. Inlaid with emeralds, lapis lazuli, and obsidian, it shimmered with an inner light, exuding an almost palpable aura. This mask would one day be known to the world as the fabled Mask of Tutankhamen.

Tutankhamen's heart thundered in his chest. He stepped forward slowly, drawn to the mask like a moth to a flame. The priests moved with precision, their actions silent and grave. Anubis, towering and composed, placed a hand on the young pharaoh's shoulder.

"You must become the observer, Tutankhamen," he said gently. "You are not the experience. You are the one who watches. From this vantage, nothing can destroy you. Remember who you truly are."

Two priests stepped forward and, with reverent care, lowered the golden mask onto Tutankhamen's head. Its interior, lined with emerald stones, pressed coolly against his skin. As he focused his thoughts, the gems began to glow with increasing brilliance, responding to the energy of his mind.

A flicker of doubt crossed his mind. "How should I begin? How do I reach that state of separation you spoke of?"

Anubis looked deep into the boy's eyes, weighing his words. "Begin as you would in meditation. Focus on the breath. Let it guide you inward. Peace is not found in the absence of fear but in the stillness that watches it. Maintain that stillness."

Tutankhamen closed his eyes. He breathed in deeply, slowly. As his breath deepened, his thoughts quieted. The glow from the emeralds brightened, casting waves of green light across his serene face.

Anubis nodded, satisfied. "That is it. Now—let go of all identity. You are the sky, not the storm. You are the silence, not the scream. Should you forget this, the experience will consume you."

At Anubis's signal, four priests lifted the granite lid and lowered it with a heavy thud onto the sarcophagus. The sound echoed like thunder. The chamber fell into perfect darkness.

Then came the pounding. Deep, resonant drums shook the air, vibrating through the stone. A chant rose in a language lost to the winds of time—raw, guttural, ancient. The scent of sacred incense filled the room, a thick, heady perfume that blurred the line between the physical and the spiritual.

Inside the sarcophagus, Tutankhamen lay cocooned in darkness. The green light from the mask pulsed in rhythm with the drums, bathing him in a verdant glow. The beat of the world outside faded until there was only breath, only light, only the journey within.

And so, the final test began.

Alone in the sacred tomb of the Great Pyramid, a boy-king entered the crucible of his soul, armed with only his will—and the power to see beyond fear.

3

After four unrelenting years immersed in research, diving headfirst into the tangled web of psychology, neuroscience, philosophy, and mysticism, I found myself standing at the crossroads where science and spirituality meet—an ancient boundary shrouded in controversy. It was the same intersection that great minds like William James and Carl Jung had quietly approached but rarely dared to cross outright. This was no place for the faint of heart. Here, in this elusive no man's land, religion and psychology engaged in an eternal, often bitter tug-of-war—one side clinging to belief, the other to empirical evidence.

I knew I had to proceed with caution. My mission was not to take sides, but to find the truth. I wasn't interested in becoming a crusader for either camp. What I was after was a remedy—a cure for the gnawing emptiness that had carved a hollow inside me since the loss of my wife, Sara, and our daughter, Christina. I believed in a Creator, yes, but I also trusted science and its ruthless pursuit of what could be proven. Somehow, I hoped the two could coexist.

When I first encountered the ancient mystery schools' teachings, I felt as if I had uncovered a forgotten world. These weren't superstitions wrapped in incense smoke and obscure ritual. No, what I had found was something altogether different—a stunningly complex mental technology, wrapped in symbolism, encoded in architecture, and buried in myth. Their methods for inducing change in consciousness were nothing short of genius. Techniques from thousands of years ago echoed in today's therapeutic practices, suggesting the ancients' understanding of the mind had been far ahead of their time.

The deeper I delved, the clearer it became: these mystery schools were the birthplaces of the world's earliest scientists and philosophers. Their teachings formed the scaffolding of a universal science that had shaped generations of enlightened minds. As I traced their legacy through history, I discovered a roll call of names so impactful, they had long since transcended mortality—luminaries whose influence had bent the arc of human knowledge and culture.

These towering figures of history had all been students of the ancient code. I became convinced that their brilliance wasn't a coincidence, but the product of something profound they had come to understand. At the heart of the mystery schools' teachings were mathematical patterns—unchanging and eternal. Pi. The Golden Ratio. The Fibonacci sequence. These weren't just numbers; they were the fingerprints of the divine, etched into the bones of reality.

These sacred figures could be found in everything: the spirals of galaxies, the geometry of flowers, the proportions of sacred architecture, and even within the chambers of the Great Pyramid. They had encoded this knowledge in stone, enduring for millennia. The mystery schools didn't view their teachings as mystical guesswork but as scientific truths rooted in universal laws. I began to believe they had developed mental disciplines aligned with this mathematical harmony—a kind of internal geometry of the soul.

Could understanding these numbers open the mind in ways never before conceived? Was this the secret that had propelled these ancient thinkers to greatness? These questions gripped me like a fever. I needed to share what I had found, but I also knew it would sound insane to most.

That's why I called Michael.

Michael had always been my anchor. A loyal friend and a hard-nosed realist, he was my check against delusion. We agreed to meet at our usual place—a modern, industrial-chic coffee shop perched on the third floor of a brick building in downtown Salt Lake City. From our table, nestled beside a massive glass window, we could see the whole valley stretching toward the horizon. Inside, the polished concrete floors gleamed beneath the soft hum of conversation. The space was filled with brushed steel and thick slabs of dark granite. The air was thick with the scent of roasted coffee and ambition.

When I arrived, Michael was already seated, a cappuccino steaming in front of him. As I approached, I felt a strange cocktail of excitement and apprehension stirring in my gut. I knew he would be skeptical. Hell, I would be too if I were him.

We exchanged small talk, but it was clear he sensed my anticipation. When I finally launched into my theory, his eyebrows lifted as if I'd just proposed we colonize the moon with alchemists. I told him everything—about the code, the temples, the names I had uncovered, the ancient mental science that had been hidden in plain sight. I watched his expression shift from polite interest to weary disbelief.

"John," he said, exasperated, "you do realize this is the same fight that's been raging forever? Science versus religion? You can't win this. No one can."

"I'm not trying to win," I replied. "I just think … maybe both sides are right. Maybe that's the point."

Michael leaned back in his chair and crossed his arms, his skepticism now radiating like heat. "If these mystery schools had such powerful secrets, why haven't they been revealed? Why all the secrecy?"

"Because they had to be secretive," I said. "Those were dangerous times. In an age where heresy could mean death, their truths had to be buried in allegory and code. Their discoveries were powerful, and power misused is always feared."

He paused, and I could see the gears turning. My words had struck a chord, but he wasn't ready to say so. Instead, he redirected the challenge.

"Even if you're right, how do you expect to uncover this so-called code? You said it yourself: Nothing was ever written down. It's a dead language, buried under thousands of years of metaphor and myth."

He was right. It was an impossible task. But I couldn't shake the conviction that this path—as insane as it appeared—was the one I was meant to follow. If this code truly held the key to unlocking the mind's potential, I had to try. I owed that much to Sara and Christina. And to myself.

Michael knew me, too well. As we stood to leave, he sighed, defeated, shaking his head.

"You're going to do this no matter what I say, aren't you?"

I smiled faintly.

He scoffed. "Well, you're going to need a few miracles if you're going to pull this off."

The word lingered in the air as we stepped into the golden light of the late afternoon. I turned it over in my mind, savoring its weight. A miracle. A chain of events that defied logic, untethered from probability. And suddenly, I realized:

Maybe miracles weren't as rare as we thought. Maybe they were simply the patterns we hadn't yet learned to see.

4

E ver since I had stumbled upon what I believed to be the core code of the ancient mystery schools, Egypt had taken hold of my mind with an almost supernatural grip. My waking hours were consumed by research into the Great Pyramid, and by night, my dreams were hijacked by visions so vivid and uncanny they seemed to bleed into reality. These weren't the idle musings of a restless mind; they were living experiences, drenched in color, feeling, and an eerie sense of truth. Often, I awoke breathless, my skin cold with sweat, my heart racing as if I had just returned from a realm more real than my own.

Each night, the line between dream and reality grew thinner. My subconscious began offering insights I had never reached through study alone. Answers to complex problems appeared in flashes of intuitive brilliance, as though whispered by unseen forces. I felt I was peeling back layers of an ancient veil, approaching the elusive meaning of the code. And yet each time I thought I had arrived, the answer I grasped seemed too simple, almost childlike in its clarity. Could something so profound truly be so elegantly obvious?

As the months passed, my dreams deepened. I no longer acted in them but observed them, as though watching an ancient reel of a life that once belonged to me. These weren't ordinary dreams; they were immersive memories, hauntingly familiar. And then, one night, everything changed. I watched myself living another life, one that felt more like home than the waking world.

In that dream, I stood in a cavernous chamber made of polished, black granite that shimmered as if alive. The air was heavy with mystery, and shadows danced along the stone walls like ancient spirits performing forgotten rites. A man cloaked in a flowing black linen robe, his face obscured by the dim glow of flickering torches, stood beside a sarcophagus that gleamed like obsidian. He motioned for me to enter.

Around us stood twelve hooded figures draped in white silk, forming a perfect circle around the sarcophagus. Though I could not see their faces, I could feel their eyes on me—glowing with an unnatural green light from within the hoods. The sight of them sent a chill through my spine. They weren't just men; they were something else, something ancient and unknowable.

I climbed into the sarcophagus, my body trembling as I lay down. The man in black began to speak, his voice resonating through the chamber like a sacred chant. It wasn't just sound; it was energy, and I felt it pull me into the body I had been observing. I was no longer watching—I was inside, reliving it.

Suddenly, a searing green light erupted above me, so intense it blinded me. Heat radiated in waves, focused on my face, until it felt as though my skin might burn away. I tried to raise my hands, to shield myself, but I met only resistance—cold, metallic, and unyielding. Trapped. I gasped for breath. Panic clawed at my chest.

Then, through the storm of fear, the black-robed man's voice came like a whisper etched in gold:

"You must learn to recognize you exist above and beyond the effects of your circumstances. You must release yourself from the habit of identifying with them. Until you do so, you will continue to allow your circumstances to determine the quality of your experience."

His voice faded into a hum, and the green light surged, overwhelming everything.

Then—silence. Utter stillness. The air turned thick and stale. A metallic tang of copper mixed with the scent of worn leather filled my nostrils. I felt buried, entombed in stillness.

Suddenly, a boom echoed through the chamber, shaking the walls with violent tremors. Another followed. The stone around me trembled like it might shatter. Was I in the middle of a battle? An earthquake? I could do nothing but brace myself, my thoughts spinning with dread.

The man's words returned, whispering through the chaos: *Calm yourself. Remember who you are.*

In an instant, I was no longer in the chamber.

I found myself under a scorching sun, its brutal light crashing down on me. As my vision adjusted, I recognized the wide, sandy expanse of a desert valley—a place I had studied endlessly. Towering before me were the pyramids, silent and eternal. Yet something was wrong. The air vibrated with tension. My sight blurred with a greenish hue, a remnant of the sarcophagus light.

Then I heard it—a cacophony of screams, crashing, chaos. I turned to see a massive crowd surging toward me. Their faces twisted in rage, their eyes hollow with madness. From my vantage point atop a stone fortress, I watched as they destroyed everything in their path, their fury unstoppable.

The crowd swarmed like locusts. Walls crumbled beneath them. Blood flowed in the dust. The soldiers guarding the perimeter fought desperately, their armor flashing in the sun, their swords swinging ceaselessly. But it was no use. For every attacker who fell, another emerged, heedless of death, charging forward with fevered rage.

These were not ordinary men. Their skin was riddled with grotesque red boils and open sores, signs of a plague that had twisted their bodies and minds. A sick horror crept over me as I realized what I was witnessing—a civilization in its death throes, lost to disease and madness.

Then came the scream—a sound so piercing, so raw, it cut through the violence like a blade.

I turned.

And there she was.

Sara.

Her eyes wide with terror, her voice lost in the roar of destruction, her presence surreal against the nightmare unfolding. My heart surged, but before I could reach her, the mob descended. The stone beneath my feet gave way as I was engulfed in a tide of writhing bodies and madness.

Then—darkness.

The dream ended. But I did not wake up the same.

I had seen too much. And somewhere in the deepest part of me, I knew it wasn't a dream at all.

5

Two weeks had passed since I experienced the vivid dream that had shown me Sara in ancient Egypt—a dream so immersive it lingered in my senses like the echo of a memory. I hadn't had any disturbing dreams since, and for that, I was grateful. But the weight of that vision still clung to me, quietly pressing against the edges of my thoughts.

In the meantime, I had buried myself in research, determined to decode the mystery that had captured my every waking hour. This elusive cipher—woven through the architecture, symbolism, and proportions of the Great Pyramid—felt omnipresent. It haunted me. No matter how many directions I approached it from, no matter how many sleepless nights I spent poring over diagrams and ancient texts, I always circled back to the same maddening conclusion: The answer was too simple.

But how could that be?

Why would the creators of the Great Pyramid—a monument so staggering in its complexity and precision—go to such extraordinary lengths to preserve a message so seemingly straightforward? If this code was truly the cornerstone of their design, then it must have held a meaning of monumental importance. And yet, I couldn't make sense of it. The simplicity mocked me. It was like staring at a lock and realizing the key had been in your pocket the whole time—yet somehow, it still didn't turn.

I knew this pattern well. Whenever I felt the grip of frustration tighten, the best thing I could do was step away. I've learned over time that my mind is most fertile when it's unburdened—when it's allowed to wander. My greatest insights often arrive in the quiet spaces between thought, when I'm focused on something entirely unrelated.

And so, I decided to stop pressing.

It had snowed heavily the night before in the quiet mountain valley where I live. Thick blankets of white clung to every rooftop and tree branch, and the roads shimmered with a deceptive gloss of ice. Driving was dangerous, but thankfully, my four-wheel drive SUV is built like a tank, and I wasn't about to let the weather trap me inside. I needed movement. I needed space to breathe.

My gym is housed in a cavernous, 20,000-square-foot warehouse—the largest of its kind in North America. It's a sensory explosion of steel, rubber, and color, packed with hundreds of gleaming machines and cutting-edge fitness equipment. Neon accents glow beneath industrial lighting, giving the place an otherworldly, almost futuristic feel. There's a rhythm to it all—the clank of weights, the hum of treadmills, the pulse of music thudding through the air.

I've been a member for more than a decade. I know every corner of that building, every creak of the floor and flicker of the overhead fluorescents. And because I loathe crowds, I always come during off-hours. On this particular day, the midday lull had left the gym nearly empty. Perfect.

After finishing my weight training, I made my way to the cardio section. Row after row of treadmills stood in silent formation, each one topped with its own small television. I usually tune them out, preferring to lose myself in music. But that day, a flickering screen caught my eye. National Geographic. Egypt. The Great Pyramid. My heart skipped a beat.

I slipped on the headphones attached to the console. Only the final ten minutes of the program remained, but I was instantly captivated. The subtitles had been left on—thank God—because the low gym music would've drowned out the audio. As the images flickered across the screen, I felt a strange electricity stir in my chest.

An Egyptologist was being interviewed. He spoke with clarity and passion about the pyramid's mysterious origin and proposed function. Then came a question that made my breath catch:

"What do you personally believe was the true purpose of the Great Pyramid?"

His answer struck me like a thunderclap:

"I believe the pyramids were used as temples by the mystery schools. There were over 200 temples in the Nile Valley, each one focused on cultivating a different aspect of being. As initiates advanced, they moved from temple to temple. The Great Pyramid, I believe, was the final step—a place where the last three exercises required to achieve adept status were completed."

Goosebumps erupted across my arms. This was the very conclusion I had been circling for weeks, doubting its simplicity, doubting myself. But here it was, voiced by a respected scholar on a nationally broadcast program.

The host, clearly intrigued, pressed further:

"What do you make of the mathematical code embedded in the pyramid's design—the numbers you've spoken about before?"

The Egyptologist smiled.

"When we examine Pi, the Golden Mean, and the Fibonacci sequence—all of which are encoded within the pyramid's geometry—we must understand that these numbers form the foundation of life itself. They are not random. They are the Universe's DNA—the blueprint of creation.

"Our ancestors believed the Universal Source to be a form of energy, and from their perspective, these codes were not merely mathematical; they were sacred. By embedding this divine blueprint into their sacred structures, they weren't just honoring the Universe—they were mirroring it. Creating a harmonious reflection of the spiritual within the physical.

"This is why their temples were built at energetic hotspots—places teeming with natural forces. In their eyes, they were crafting environments where the spiritual and the physical could coexist in perfect equilibrium. The Great Pyramid wasn't just a monument—it was a sanctuary, a vessel of divine resonance."

The host was momentarily speechless. So was I.

This man had just articulated—word for word—the intuitive conclusions I had agonized over in solitude. I had been right. Balance. Harmony. The alignment of the physical and the spiritual. But what did it mean in practical terms? Why had this been so central to the teachings of the mystery schools? Why had so much been devoted to preserving this knowledge?

As the credits rolled, one last image flickered across the screen: the King's Chamber, bathed in the warm glow of torchlight, the red granite sarcophagus at its heart pulsing with silent mystery.

I stood there in stunned silence.

What were the odds that I would catch that specific program—during that specific moment—on a day I had almost stayed home?

Needless to say, I left the gym in a daze, my thoughts spinning, my spirit stirred. I hardly ever watch TV, let alone stumble onto divine synchronicities. But something had shifted. I could feel it.

The code's meaning hadn't changed.

But now—I had begun to understand *why* it mattered.

6

Romantic relationships have never come easily to me. It takes something extraordinary, something undeniable, to truly capture my attention. With Sara, it had been exactly that—a moment so powerful it etched itself into the very architecture of my memory. The first time I laid eyes on her, it was as though the world paused mid-breath. Time stilled, and all the ambient noise of existence softened into silence. In that instant, recognition—ancient and inexplicable—passed between us. I had never experienced anything like it, before or since.

That first encounter was like stepping out of a dream and realizing you had only just awakened. She saw me—not the curated persona I projected, not the layers I had carefully built to shield myself, but the real me. It should have terrified me, being that exposed, that vulnerable. But with Sara, vulnerability felt like safety. I couldn't hide from her, and for once, I didn't want to. After something so rare and sacred, I could no longer accept anything less. Not in love.

So, when I arrived late one wintry afternoon to meet Michael for coffee at our usual spot, romance was the furthest thing from my mind. I was still haunted by my dream of Sara and preoccupied with the puzzle of the ancient code. The air outside was sharp with cold, and a thick ceiling of iron-gray clouds blanketed the valley, muting the sunlight and plunging the city into premature dusk. The coffee shop glowed like a refuge of warmth and humanity against the bleakness of the weather.

Inside, the place was unusually packed for that hour of the day. Maybe it was the oppressive sky or the winter inversion common in Salt Lake that drove people indoors seeking heat, comfort, and caffeine. The scent of roasted beans and cinnamon lingered like a warm blanket in the air. As I stood in line, I spotted Michael already settled at our usual table near the window, flipping through his newspaper as if he'd claimed the seat hours ago.

The line moved swiftly, and soon I found myself face-to-face with Rachel. She was radiant—light brown hair tucked beneath a knit beanie, eyes the color of glacier ice. She greeted me with her usual easy charm, her smile warm and inviting. I had seen her many times before, and though I had always found her attractive, I had never considered her in a romantic light. But today, something was different.

We exchanged a few words about the weather, and then she launched into a recounting of yesterday's drama at the shop—a heated altercation that ended with a cup of scalding coffee thrown across the room. It was almost laughably out of place in a café frequented by philosophers, artists, and mellowed-out hippies. Alex, one of the regulars, had apparently pushed someone too far during one of his infamous business pitches. According to Rachel, a running joke among the staff was that Alex lured unsuspecting victims into a multi-level marketing scheme.

Then she said it.

"I think it's a pyramid scheme."

My heart lurched.

The word "pyramid" hit me like a thunderclap. It dragged me back into the heart of my dream, into the sands of Egypt, to Sara's eyes beneath a linen veil and the Great Pyramid's towering geometry. I froze. My thoughts went blank, my tongue stuck in place, my mind spinning in a vortex of ancient symbols and lingering emotion.

"John?" Rachel asked, leaning in. "Are you okay? You look like you've seen a ghost."

"Oh!" I stammered, too loudly. "A pyramid scheme?"

She blinked at me, startled by the volume, then offered a tentative laugh. "Yeah … Confederated Products, I think. It's not an actual pyramid scheme, just one of those … you know, multi-level deals."

I nodded, trying to regain my composure, though my mind remained firmly anchored in the sands of Giza. I thanked her quickly and shuffled over to Michael, who hadn't looked up from his paper.

But the moment I sat down, he folded the pages and gave me a knowing look.

"You ought to ask her out, John," he said flatly. "She likes you."

I offered my usual brush-off. "You think so? I hadn't noticed. I'll think about it."

Michael rarely pushed when I gave him that line, but today, he leaned in.

"You deserve to be happy. Sara would want that. She wouldn't want to see you this way."

His words hit me harder than I had expected. He was right. Sara wouldn't want to see me this way—caught between dreams and shadows, clinging to something I could never get back. But I wasn't ready. Not yet. Something was still unfolding, something just beneath the surface, and I knew Sara was somehow still a part of it.

"Actually," I said, shifting the conversation, "speaking of Sara, I had the strangest dream recently …."

I went on to tell him everything—the dream, the symbols, the sense of divine connection. But as I spoke, I could see Michael's patience fraying. His expression remained neutral, but tension radiated from him.

When I finally paused for breath, he cut in.

"Have you ever considered that maybe you're seeing this stuff because you want to? You've been obsessed for years, John. Maybe it's time to let go."

A heavy silence fell between us. He picked up his paper again, his way of retreating.

And then, just as quickly as he had closed off, he opened again.

"You've got to be kidding me," he said suddenly. "This might be your lucky week. Have you seen what's coming to the Salt Palace?"

He flipped the paper around and pointed to an ad. My breath caught in my throat.

King Tut.

The world-renowned exhibit would be in Salt Lake City in just two weeks.

Michael and I stared at each other, equally stunned.

"Looks like you might not need to go to Egypt after all," he said, his voice tinged with irony. "Maybe Egypt's coming to you."

For the first time in days, a flicker of hope lit within me. Maybe, just maybe, this was more than a coincidence. Maybe I hadn't imagined the connection. Maybe there really was something waiting to be discovered, and perhaps—just perhaps—Sara was guiding me there.

7

The night air bit through my coat as Michael and I stood shivering outside the Salt Palace, our breaths forming clouds that danced above the crowd. We had chosen—perhaps unwisely—to attend the opening night of the King Tutankhamun exhibit. It was bitter cold, and the line to get in was endless, stretching like a frozen serpent down the narrow alleyway, crammed with bodies and buzzing with impatient energy. The crowd pressed close, shoulder to shoulder, and the narrowness of the space only intensified the suffocating closeness.

Restlessness swirled inside me, a tight knot of anticipation and unease. I couldn't tell if the anxiety stemmed from the sheer density of people packed into the alley or from some deeper, inexplicable sense that something was about to happen. My gut tugged at me with a strange warning I couldn't decipher.

Trying to distract myself from the growing claustrophobia, I began explaining my sensitivity to crowds to Michael—something I rarely ever spoke about. It wasn't fear or social anxiety. I wasn't antisocial. It was something different, something more invasive. Being close to large groups of people overwhelmed me, not physically but emotionally. Like a sponge, I absorbed the surrounding emotional energy—grief, joy, anger, and fear. In small groups, I could manage it. But in tightly packed crowds like this one, it became unbearable, like drowning in a sea of unnamed feelings that weren't mine but that I felt just the same.

Sara had never understood. My empathic behavior had become one of the silent wedges in our relationship. I had tried to explain, but she had always seen it as an excuse or a weakness. Michael, on the other hand, listened in his usual pragmatic way, his breath curling in the frigid air.

"Just turn it off, John. Ignore it. Other people's problems are not yours."

I almost laughed. If only it were that simple. If only there were a switch. Then maybe I could move through life without being pummeled by invisible waves of emotion everywhere I went.

After what felt like an eternity, we finally shuffled through the entrance into the blessed warmth of the Salt Palace. The interior was alive with the excited murmurs of hundreds of visitors, their voices bouncing off the high ceilings. I could feel the collective awe as we neared the exhibit's entrance. Warmth returned to my limbs, but the buzzing in my head remained.

The first thing we saw was an enormous golden plaque bearing the name Howard Carter. His discovery of Tutankhamun's tomb in 1922 had become legendary. Unlike the plundered graves of other pharaohs, Tut's tomb had been found sealed and intact. And with that discovery came whispered tales of a curse.

I recounted to Michael the strange events said to have followed—the sudden, mysterious illness that had taken the life of Lord Carnarvon shortly after he had entered the tomb, and the bizarre death of Carter's pet bird, killed by a cobra that had slithered into his quarters.

Locals, steeped in superstition, believed the tomb had been cursed to protect it from intrusion.

Michael scoffed. "There's way too much room for coincidence here, John. You don't actually believe the curse was real, do you?"

"I'm not sure what to believe," I replied. "I just love the mystery of it all."

He shook his head with an amused smirk. "Someday, John, I'll cure you of all your superstitions."

The exhibit was breathtaking. Ancient artifacts glowed under spotlights: glimmering scarabs, intricately painted jars, jewelry still bright with color. Each piece spoke of unimaginable craftsmanship and devotion to a belief system long buried beneath the sands of time. Visitors young and old moved reverently among the displays, their faces aglow with wonder.

And yet, as we moved from case to case, I couldn't shake a sense of disappointment. I'd expected something more—something to tie these ancient relics to the dreams I'd been having about the mystery schools. I had hoped for a sign, a moment of recognition or connection. But nothing came.

That is, until we reached the final display.

The golden death mask of Tutankhamen gleamed beneath a spotlight, so vivid and lifelike it seemed to radiate an energy all its own. The moment my eyes met the mask, a piercing pain shot through my skull. It lanced down my spine, crashing like a wave through my entire body. My legs buckled.

The world tilted. I reached for something—anything—to steady myself, but there was nothing. I collapsed, and everything went black.

When I opened my eyes, I was no longer in the Salt Palace.

I was walking down a sandstone-colored corridor, surrounded by men in flowing white silk robes. The air was warm and thick with incense. We moved in silence, following a regal figure ahead of us. He wore a red silk robe and a gold-jeweled crown and held a white ivory staff. I knew him—though not from this life. He was the same man I'd seen in my dreams.

We ascended the sloping corridor known as the Grand Gallery inside the Great Pyramid. Each step echoed softly as we climbed the rough-hewn stone. Golden brackets held glowing white stones on the walls, illuminating the narrow passage with an ethereal light.

Then I noticed her.

Sara walked beside me, her hand in mine. How had I not seen her before? She wore a radiant white robe, her eyes full of knowing. I wanted to speak but found myself unable to. Her presence alone stilled my questions.

In the Queen's Chamber, a white granite sarcophagus sat at the center. I didn't recognize it. This wasn't something I had ever read about—this sarcophagus wasn't supposed to exist. Behind it, a dark wooden table bore several sacred relics, and there, unmistakable, was Tutankhamen's mask.

Sara turned to me.

"Do not be afraid, my love," she said gently. "The exercise you are about to perform will not only benefit you; it will also have a positive impact on your people. Your actions in this moment will affect this world for centuries to come."

Before I could respond, the man in red motioned for me to step forward. The others formed a circle around the sarcophagus. As I approached, I was struck by the quiet reverence in their eyes. Two of them helped me lie down inside the stone coffin.

Then came the mask.

Two men approached, bearing the golden mask. My chest tightened. They lowered it over my head, and the weight of it consumed me—crushing, suffocating. Panic surged.

I wanted to scream, to tear it off, to flee this impossible vision. But then I heard her voice.

"Do not be afraid, my love. All will be well."

Her voice was soft and certain. I clung to it.

Then, in an instant, her face was gone, replaced by another—Michael's. His eyes were wide with fear, his face just inches from mine.

"John! Are you with me, John? Stay with me, buddy! Help is on the way! You're going to be just fine!"

The golden light faded. The Queen's Chamber disappeared. The cold tile floor of the Salt Palace pressed against my back.

Later, Michael told me that I had collapsed, suddenly and without warning. He said I'd been calling out to Sara—begging her not to leave me.

Even now, I'm not sure what I experienced. A vision? A dream? A memory from another life? All I know is that I saw her. I felt her hand in mine. And I heard her voice telling me we were forever bound. And in my heart, I believe her.

8

In the wake of my experience at the Salt Palace, I found myself revisiting the same emotional and intellectual terrain I thought I had already charted. But now, with a renewed sense of clarity, I realized something I hadn't before: Sara had been woven into every thread of my journey into Egypt and the ancient mystery schools. Her presence, once warm and physical, had transformed into a haunting echo that followed me with unwavering persistence.

Ever since I'd stood before the golden mask—its ancient aura awakening something dormant within me—my dreams became a nightly pilgrimage into an Egypt that felt less like a fantasy and more like a veiled memory. Each dream brought with it vivid landscapes, cryptic symbols, and, always, Sara. I couldn't outrun her. Her ghost lingered like incense smoke in the corner of my mind—comforting, yet suffocating. The dreams left me emotionally exhausted, blurring the lines between grief and revelation. What had started as a desperate search to cope with her loss had transformed into a sacred path, one where every step forward drew me closer to the realization that she had never truly left.

A week after the Salt Palace encounter, I had a dream that eclipsed all the others in clarity and intensity. I was back in ancient Egypt, seated on the balcony of a sandstone compound that overlooked the Nile. The structure was familiar, a recurring symbol in my dreams, once under siege, now serene.

The air was rich with life. Above me stretched an endless canopy of crystal-clear azure sky. The sun's warmth wrapped around me like a silken shawl, tender and healing. The river shimmered below, its waters whispering secrets in a language just beyond comprehension. In the distance, the pyramids rose like timeless sentinels—colossal, precise, and impossibly ancient. But what struck me most was the landscape. Where I expected an arid desert, I instead saw lush fields swaying with dark green crops. Palm trees lined the banks of the river, and the scent of blooming lotus drifted on a warm breeze, perfumed with something strangely familiar.

It was that scent that turned my head.

And there she was.

Sara sat to my right, beneath an elegantly woven awning, in a dark wooden chair carved with intricate patterns. She looked entirely at peace. The chair creaked gently as she shifted to face me. My breath caught in my throat. I had wanted this—longed for it with every cell of my being—but now that it was here, I was paralyzed by the weight of everything unsaid.

When I finally managed to speak, the words tumbled from my lips like fragile glass.

"I miss you. You took a part of me with you when you died. Life hasn't been the same. I've been carrying this emptiness around, and I don't know how to let go."

She said nothing at first. Just watched me with those piercing blue eyes—eyes that always seemed to understand more than they let on. She listened with a stillness that made the world around us fade. When I finished, she leaned forward slightly, her gaze never wavering.

"You must understand, my love," she said, her voice like velvet stretched across the centuries, "you and I are part of a greater plan. I had to leave this world so you could rediscover who you truly are."

The words lodged in my heart like a key turning in a long-forgotten lock.

I blinked, struggling to take it in. "Why did you have to leave for me to rediscover myself?"

Her face softened with sorrow, and tears glistened in her eyes. "I didn't want to. But you were losing yourself in the illusion of this lifetime. You had begun to identify only with your present circumstances. You are meant for more than that. Your soul is ancient. You are beginning to remember."

She paused, as if waiting for me to absorb the magnitude of her words.

"A greater identity is inside you," she continued. "One that holds the essence of all the lifetimes you've lived. Through the process of awakening, you'll begin to reconnect with the gifts and truths you've carried for centuries."

I nodded slowly, trying to piece together the fragments.

"Are you saying these dreams are memories from past lives?" I asked. "What am I supposed to do with them?"

Sara reached out and took my hand. Her touch felt real—warm and grounding. "You're only at the beginning. To reclaim your full identity, you must undergo training—training that began many lifetimes ago and was interrupted. That's why you're drawn to the mystery schools and their hidden code. You left a message for yourself."

"Where do I go for this training?"

She smiled gently, as though I had asked something obvious. "To Egypt, of course. You must return to where it all began. The temples, the pyramids—they are more than monuments. They are mirrors of the soul. You once said the message needed to be left in plain sight. You helped shape it—balance and harmony encoded in stone so that when the time was right, you would remember."

My thoughts swirled. Had I played a role in building the temples? In creating the very message I now sought to decode?

"What is the message?" I asked. "What does it mean?"

Her eyes clouded, tinged with sadness. "How could you forget? It was the message of balance and harmony. It's everything. It's the key to awakening, to healing the world. You'll understand more as you remember. But before I go, there is one more thing you must know."

She stood then, her form shimmering slightly in the golden light of the dreamscape.

"Your task is vital. The fate of humanity rests, in part, on your shoulders. You are not alone—your companions from past lifetimes will find you. Trust the process. Listen to your inner voice. Everything you need is already within you."

As she finished speaking, the dream dissolved around me like morning mist. I awoke in my apartment, my heart pounding with purpose.

I knew what I had to do.

I had to go to Egypt.

But the reality of my life came crashing back. I was broke. Years of focused research had drained my finances. I had no idea how I would make the journey happen.

All I knew was this: If I were ever to find the answers, I needed a miracle.

9

Just a few days after I had resolved, with unwavering conviction, to travel to Egypt in search of answers, I decided to confide in Michael. I told him plainly that I felt Egypt held the key to unraveling the mysteries that had begun to unfold in my life. He chuckled the moment I said it. Of course he did. He knew all too well that my financial state was, to put it kindly, less than ideal. In his eyes, Egypt was just a dream—a far-off, sun-drenched mirage on the edge of a desert I had no means to cross.

Two weeks had passed. Then came that Saturday morning.

I awoke to a furious ringing at my front door. The noise tore through the veil of sleep like a siren, jarring and relentless. My eyes flew open, and I groaned, immediately irritated. It was only 7 a.m., and anyone who truly knew me would understand how unholy an hour that was for a Saturday. I am not, nor have I ever been, a morning person.

The bell rang again, then again—a persistent, shrill chorus that shredded any hope of returning to sleep. With a heavy sigh, I dragged myself from the warmth of my bed, feeling the chill of the morning air on my skin. My limbs were slow, my thoughts still tangled in the remnants of dreams. I slipped on a shirt, muttering under my breath as I stumbled toward the door.

I paused at the peephole, expecting to find someone—perhaps Michael with some ill-timed joke or an overly enthusiastic delivery driver. But the hallway was silent, completely empty. I frowned and opened the door, the hinges groaning softly.

That's when I saw it.

A single FedEx envelope sat on the doormat like a fallen message from another realm. No one was in sight. The air outside was still, cool, and oddly expectant—as though it, too, was holding its breath.

I picked up the envelope and turned it over in my hands. My eyes caught a name printed neatly on the shipping label, and my heart skipped a beat.

David Bruce.

It was a name I hadn't thought about in years. Years ago, I had invested $30,000 with David's financial firm, just before the world was thrown into chaos by the greatest financial disaster since the Great Depression. When the dust settled, David's name had been splashed across headlines. Fraud. Scandal. Collapse. I had wanted to believe he was innocent, that the man I'd trusted had been caught in a storm not of his own making.

But then Sara and Christina were taken from me in the same tragic year, and the money no longer mattered. My grief swallowed everything.

My fingers trembled slightly as I tore open the envelope. Inside, there were two items: a letter, handwritten in a deliberate and familiar hand, and a check. When I unfolded the check, I gasped. $50,000. The room blurred as tears welled up in my eyes. I sank onto the nearest chair, clutching the letter like a lifeline.

In his letter, David spoke with humility and grace. He apologized for his silence, for the years that had passed without a word. He told me he had lost everything during the collapse, that he had come within inches of ruin. But somehow, he had clawed his way back, rebuilding his life from the ashes.

What struck me most were his words about me. He said he had never forgotten that I was the only investor who hadn't pursued legal action against him. That gesture had stayed with him, haunted him in the best possible way. He said it had given him hope. And now, he was returning not just my original investment, but more—a gesture of gratitude, and, in his words, a small piece of redemption.

He ended the letter with something that cracked my heart wide open: "I have faith you will rediscover those aspects of yourself you've lost. May this help you on your journey."

In that moment, I felt the boundaries of logic and coincidence dissolve. This was more than a check. It was a sign. A miracle. Just when the path ahead seemed blocked by the sheer weight of impossibility, the Universe had delivered a key. Egypt was no longer a distant dream. It was real. It was calling.

And now, I could finally answer.

10

Before calling Michael, I decided to have a little fun with him. The joy from my recent good fortune buzzed through my veins like champagne bubbles, and I couldn't resist the opportunity to toy with him. Michael, the eternal skeptic, never failed to find a rational explanation for the inexplicable events shaping my life lately. Where I saw miracles, he saw coincidence. Where I felt divine intervention, he saw random chance. I was eager to see how he'd rationalize this one.

I dialed his number with a grin tugging at the corners of my mouth, imagining his face twisting in disbelief. I was practically giddy, curious to hear the gymnastics his mind would perform trying to explain away the latest turn of events.

The moment he answered, I dove in. "Hey, Michael, just wanted to let you know … I'm going to Egypt. I bought my tickets this morning."

There was a beat of silence on the line, and then, just as I expected, he exploded.

"What?! You've completely lost it this time, John. How the hell are you paying for that? It's not like you've been raking in paychecks! I can't remember the last time you had a steady job."

He wasn't wrong. My financial state had been tenuous at best. Over the last few years, I'd lived modestly, forced to stretch every dollar like taffy. But something in me found satisfaction in riling him up, pushing his buttons just enough to watch the steam rise.

"I can't shake the feeling that this code—this mystery—holds something vital for me," I said with a theatrical air. "I believe understanding it might be the key to healing. Egypt is where the answers are waiting. I feel … called there. I know you think it's nonsense, but this pull I feel is real."

Michael groaned audibly. I could picture him pacing in his kitchen, running a frustrated hand through his hair.

"You can't be serious, John. None of this makes sense. You're chasing phantoms. You're turning chance into prophecy."

He paused, probably hoping I'd come to my senses, but I stayed silent, letting the moment stretch. I could feel his tension building like thunderclouds ready to burst.

Then, casually, I dropped the bomb. "Did I mention I just received $50,000 this morning? Right before I called you."

A beat. Silence. Then, incredulity: "What?!"

I laughed, the sound full of mischief. "Yep. A check. Delivered to my door in a FedEx envelope. From David Bruce. Remember him? I invested thirty grand with his firm back in '08, right before everything crashed. I'd written it off years ago."

Michael's voice softened, tinged with disbelief. "You got that money back? Are you serious?"

"Dead serious," I said, my voice now calmer, awash with the same awe I'd felt earlier that morning. "David wrote me a letter. Apologized for the delay, thanked me for never taking legal action, and returned my investment with interest. Said he'd been thinking about me for years."

A long silence followed. I knew what he was doing—running the odds in his head, weighing probabilities, grasping for logic.

"John," he finally said, chuckling, "I still think you're out of your mind for taking this trip. But well played. Maybe I need to start paying more attention to my dreams. Apparently, they work. Maybe I'll dream up a new Porsche tonight."

We both laughed. Though he tried to keep up the skeptical facade, I knew him too well. Beneath the sarcasm, something in him stirred. He had seen the same shimmer of magic I had. Even if he couldn't admit it aloud, he felt it too.

And for a moment, even Michael, the die-hard realist, allowed himself to believe in miracles.

11

My flights from Salt Lake City to New York, and then onward to London, were mostly uneventful—quiet islands of time suspended between the lives I was leaving behind and the unknown road ahead. Somewhere above the inky expanse of the Atlantic Ocean, I found myself curled beneath a thin airline blanket, lulled into silence by the hum of the engines and the soft rustle of slumbering passengers around me. The plane felt like a liminal space, a no-man's-land between past and future.

I sat there in the half-light, my reflection faint in the cold oval of the airplane window, and let my mind drift through the maze of the last few years. So much loss. So much change. I had come a long way to reach this moment, yet the road ahead still felt as unfathomable as the dark waves beneath us. I was grateful, at least, that I didn't have to explain the strange reasons for my journey to any of the chatty travelers beside me. Egypt held a mystique of its own; it needed no justification. No one even asked.

When I finally landed at Heathrow, the terminal's fluorescent brightness and the crowd's motion jarred me awake. I had a two-hour layover before my connecting flight to Cairo. Hunger gnawed at me, so I decided to find one of the airport's many small cafés. As I walked past polished storefronts and bustling kiosks, the smell of fresh pastries, grilled meats, and coffee wafted from every direction. Despite the abundance of choices, I wandered aimlessly for several minutes, lost not just in indecision but in thought.

Sara's final words kept echoing in my head, their weight haunting me:

"Your task is vital. The fate of humanity rests, in part, on your shoulders. You are not alone—your companions from past lifetimes will find you. Trust the process. Listen to your inner voice. Everything you need is already within you."

What was so special about me? I felt anything but special. If anything, I had been slowly disappearing since the day I had lost Sara and Christina. Grief had stripped me bare, leaving only a husk of the man I used to be.

I remembered another lifetime—only six years earlier—when I stood under spotlights at a glittering awards ceremony, shoulder to shoulder with Michael. We had been crowned top producers of our financial firm for the fifth year running. I could still see the looks of thinly veiled envy on the faces of our colleagues, and still hear the thunder of applause as we accepted the plaques commemorating our achievements.

Back then, the phones never stopped ringing. My calendar was packed with elite social functions, invites to yacht parties, and last-minute flights to private resorts. My life had been gilded with success and saturated with superficial adoration. Michael and I had felt invincible.

And now? Now I drifted through a terminal full of strangers, an invisible man burdened with a forgotten mission. Sometimes, when I looked in the mirror, I barely recognized the eyes staring back. Where had that confident, ambitious man gone? Would he ever return?

After settling on a cozy pub nestled beside one of the departure wings, I ordered the traditional fish and chips. The familiar crunch of batter and the sharp tang of malt vinegar grounded me momentarily, but the haze returned the moment I stepped out and headed toward my gate.

The departure area for Cairo was nearly deserted, save for a handful of weary travelers sprawled across the molded seats. I made my way to a row by the wide, floor-to-ceiling windows. Outside, the weather matched my mood: Leaden skies brooded above a drizzle that streaked the glass. I took a seat close to the window, drawn to the solitude it offered.

There was something meditative about watching rain fall from behind glass—a sense of safety amid the storm. I leaned back and allowed myself to simply be. No distractions. No phone. Just the rhythmic tap of rain and the distant murmur of airport announcements.

Then I noticed him.

He sat three or four seats away, hunched inward as if the weight of the world pressed against his spine. His appearance was disheveled—a tangled mop of greasy brown hair, skin pale and slack beneath the coarse stubble on his jaw. His clothes looked slept-in and stained from days of use. He seemed to vibrate with grief and exhaustion.

Something about the way he stared at nothing captured me. His vacant eyes were filled with an aching emptiness I recognized all too well. I didn't know him, but I knew his pain.

Our eyes met, just for a second.

And in that instant, something inside me cracked open.

I felt him—his despair, his hopelessness, his longing to feel something other than numb. The emotions hit me like a wave, washing over me with such force I had to break the gaze and look away. Tears burned behind my eyes, and I swallowed hard to contain the flood.

He looked like I must have in those first raw months after losing my family. Hollow. Unmoored. Desperate to find solid ground again. A ghost wandering the world of the living.

The connection between us, however fleeting, was undeniable. I sensed that he, too, was searching for something—for meaning, for a spark, for a sliver of light to lead him out of the dark.

And yet, despite that shared recognition, I didn't approach him. His misery was a sacred space, and I knew all too well how intrusive compassion could feel when you're clinging to your last threads of control.

Instead, I turned back to the window, watching the rain blur the outside world into smears of gray.

In that moment, I knew how far I had come. I wasn't whole yet—not even close—but I was moving forward. And maybe that was enough.

12

The view from my aircraft window as we descended into Cairo was unlike anything I'd ever seen. The sky stretched endlessly above, a dome of radiant, cloudless blue that seemed to press down on the golden sea of desert below. And there, emerging from the vast, sun-bleached plain like ancient sentinels, stood the pyramids.

Even at this altitude, the Great Pyramid of Giza and its companions dominated the landscape, their sharp, angular forms rising in defiance of time itself. They cast long shadows across the sands, unmoved by centuries, untouched by the chaos of the modern city that sprawled around them. Cairo, with its vibrant pulse and tangled streets, buzzed with life beneath us, but the pyramids stood still—majestic, serene, eternal.

My heart thudded in my chest as I pressed my forehead to the cool glass. I felt as though I were flying not just over a place, but into another reality—a thin veil separating the ancient world from the present fluttered before my eyes, and for a moment, I felt it slip. I tried to imagine what the pyramids would say if they could speak. What secrets had they swallowed over the millennia? What truths had their immovable gaze witnessed? Their presence was calming, yes, but also commanding—like being in the company of gods.

The message of balance and harmony embedded in their geometry echoed in my mind. Was it more than symbolism? Was it a code, a calling, something my soul had always recognized but never truly understood? I didn't have the answers. Not yet.

As the plane's wheels kissed the scorching tarmac, the spell lifted slightly. The engines' thrum brought me back to myself, and with it, a rush of doubt. Had I truly been led here by something greater than myself? Was I chasing ghosts? I didn't know. All I knew was I had come this far on what felt like a thread of destiny. Despite the doubts clawing at the edges of my resolve, a deep part of me still believed I had to be here.

The plane taxied slowly to the gate. I exhaled, realizing I'd been holding my breath. My body ached from the long journey, but the exhaustion couldn't dull the rising anticipation. I gathered my things and stood, swaying slightly as I pulled my carry-on from the overhead bin. My feet were eager to touch the earth of Egypt, the cradle of civilization, the land of secrets.

As I shuffled with the others through the narrow aisle and out into the terminal, I tried to steady myself, to shake off the strange mix of excitement and unease.

Then, from the corner of my eye, I saw him.

That same broken man from Heathrow. There he was, unmistakable, drifting like a ghost through the terminal, his form hunched, his pace brisk. He was a hundred yards ahead, and I surged forward instinctively. Something pulled at me, urging me to catch up. But the crowd was thick and sluggish, and he moved quickly, unimpeded. I weaved through people, trying to close the distance, but it was useless. He was gaining ground.

He reached the top of the stairs and turned—not toward baggage claim like the rest of us, but toward the exit. That struck me. No luggage. No hesitation. Just a single-minded departure into the unknown. Who travels halfway across the world with nothing but the clothes on their back? And yet, I knew he had a purpose. What it was, I couldn't say.

My gaze followed him until he disappeared from view. A pang of disappointment tugged at my chest. I didn't know why this stranger haunted me, but I couldn't shake the sense that we were connected—that some thread linked our paths together.

While I stood waiting for my bag, my eyes drifted to the terminal's glass wall. Outside, the heat was already shimmering off the pavement, turning the air into a restless, wavering mirage. A line of yellow, black, and white taxis idled at the curb, their drivers slouched inside, soaked with sweat, faces glistening under the sun's harsh glare. Even their air conditioners seemed to strain against the furnace-like heat.

Movement in the corner of my eye made me turn. Toward the back of the taxi line, I spotted him again. The man. He was sliding into the backseat of a yellow cab, his face turned away. As soon as the door shut, the car peeled away from the curb and vanished into the city's labyrinth.

I stood still, unnerved and strangely hollow. What was this strange gravity he had over me? Why did he seem to be everywhere I turned?

My bag finally arrived. I slung it over my shoulder and made my way to the curb, where my hotel shuttle waited. I climbed aboard, feeling the cool rush of the air conditioning wash over my sun-warmed skin. And as the bus pulled away, heading into the city of Cairo, I heard her voice again.

"You will only find the answers you are seeking in Egypt."

Sara's words echoed through my mind, sharp and undeniable. A chill danced up my spine despite the desert heat. I didn't know what I was looking for anymore—answers, healing, some long-lost connection to Sara, or even to myself. Maybe all of it. Maybe none of it. All I knew was that I had arrived. And now, all that remained was to see what would unfold.

13

Other than the driver, I was the only passenger in the hotel shuttle that morning. The vehicle itself was a gleaming, school-bus-sized coach, its wide, empty seats and echoing cabin making its vastness feel almost surreal. It seemed excessive that such a large bus had traveled all the way from the city just to retrieve me, a lone traveler lost in a sea of sand and sky. But after nearly twenty-four grueling hours spent shuffling through crowded airports and wedging into cramped airplane seats, I welcomed the solitude.

Inside the air-conditioned cocoon of the shuttle, silence wrapped around me like a soft blanket. The only sound was the engine's steady hum and the occasional hiss of sand against the undercarriage. I stretched my legs out in front of me, allowing myself to relax for the first time in what felt like days. My senses were wide open, drinking in every detail around me without the usual distractions of fellow travelers.

As we pulled away from the terminal and cruised along the desert highway into Cairo, the scenery unfolded like a dreamscape. Vast, sunlit stretches of golden sand extended in every direction, punctuated by the rare shrub or glint of metal from a distant vehicle. The sky overhead was a brilliant, cloudless blue, and the morning light danced across the horizon like a blessing.

And then, there they were.

Rising in the distance like giants emerging from the earth, the pyramids and the stoic Sphinx came into view. They shimmered in the heat, massive and eternal. From this ground-level vantage, they looked impossibly large—far more awe-inspiring than they had from the air. Their sharply chiseled silhouettes cut into the sky with an air of defiance, as though daring time itself to challenge their permanence.

I found myself captivated by their mystery. Even from miles away, I could make out the size of the colossal stone blocks that made up the Great Pyramid. I imagined the hands that had placed each one—the sweat, the labor, the sheer will it must have taken to give birth to something so enduring. How had the ancient Egyptians accomplished this without the machinery we take for granted today? What secrets still lay buried beneath their symmetrical surfaces?

As we neared the city's edge, the landscape transformed. The clean, open desert gave way to a living museum of narrow alleys and aged buildings. I felt as though I had been transported centuries back in time. Rows of crumbling stone structures flanked the dusty streets, their facades weathered by wind and sun. Market stalls brimming with antiques spilled into walkways, and the scent of spices, old wood, and roasted meats filled the air.

Vendors, dressed in flowing robes of muted earth tones and sun-washed colors, moved with purpose, setting up their goods for the day. Turbaned men bartered over crates of vegetables, while veiled women guided children through the maze of early-morning commerce.

The city pulsed with life—but not the modern kind. Its rhythm was rooted in history, tradition, and something ancient and unchanging.

My chest tightened with a mix of awe and anxiety. I felt like a stranger in someone else's dream, detached from the world I had always known. Just when I feared the unfamiliarity might overwhelm me, the shuttle crossed into a different part of the city, and the scene changed once more.

The hotel stood like a monument to the modern age. Its sleek, steel framework and glistening glass panels caught the sunlight like a beacon, reaching skyward for nearly thirty stories. As we rolled into the parking lot, a wave of relief washed over me. I had arrived back in a time and place I recognized.

Inside, the hotel lobby offered a stark contrast to the city streets I had just witnessed. Cool, air-conditioned air enveloped me the moment I stepped through the doors. The floors gleamed underfoot, and towering glass walls let natural light flood in, reflecting off polished steel beams. A sense of calm returned to my body.

Behind the granite front desk stood a concierge, a man in his mid-thirties with warm olive skin and kind eyes. His professional, yet friendly demeanor was a balm to my travel-wearied soul. Sensing my exhaustion, he wasted no time with small talk. Instead, he swiftly checked me in, even upgrading me to a suite on the tenth floor, free of charge.

"Enjoy your stay with us, Mr. Fullman," he said with a gracious nod. "Please let us know if there is anything you need."

I thanked him sincerely and made my way toward the elevator, my eyes drawn upward to the vast, vaulted ceiling. The entire structure had an ethereal quality, as if designed not just for comfort but to elevate the spirit. I couldn't help but wonder if the architecture had been influenced, even subtly, by the sacred geometry encoded in the pyramids.

The glass elevator climbed smoothly to the tenth floor. When I stepped into my suite, I found myself momentarily speechless. The room opened up to a breathtaking, panoramic view of the Nile Valley. Far in the distance, the Great Pyramid stood once more, resolute and radiant under the afternoon sun. It almost seemed to shimmer, beckoning me—calling me.

I knew in my bones that this place, this monument, and whatever message it guarded, were the reasons I had come. There was no more questioning. No more doubt. Only the strange certainty that something awaited me within those ancient stones.

But first, a shower.

The hot water soothed my aching muscles, washing away the grit and fatigue of my long journey. Afterward, I wrapped myself in a soft robe and set the alarm clock on the nightstand. I only had three days in Egypt—I couldn't afford to lose one of them to sleep.

As I reached to set the alarm, my fingers brushed against a small pile of brochures. They looked worn, edges frayed, likely left behind by the room's previous guests. One in particular caught my eye—a glossy, colorful trifold with the image of the Great Pyramid on its cover.

Inside was a tour schedule. One departure time, 4:30 p.m., had been circled in blue ink. A strange shiver crept over me. Was it merely coincidence—or a sign? I had long ago learned to pay attention to moments like this. They were the whispers of fate.

I set the alarm for 2:30 p.m. and lay down, letting the sheets envelope me. As sleep took hold, Sara's words echoed in my mind like a forgotten melody returning: "Only by undergoing this training will you remember your true identity."

Whatever training she had meant, whatever mystery lay hidden within the code, I knew it was waiting for me. And I would be ready.

14

As I stepped out of the hotel shuttle and onto the blistering sand-strewn asphalt outside the Great Pyramid, it felt as though I had passed through a curtain of ice into the heart of a furnace. The van's frigid air conditioning had barely left my skin before the desert heat swallowed me whole. The afternoon sun hung low but fierce, its rays slashing through the sky like molten blades, casting long angular shadows across the ancient landscape.

I squinted upward, and there it stood—Khufu's monolithic creation, impossibly massive, its sun-washed limestone blocks radiating waves of heat. I was grateful for the pyramid's bulk, which mercifully shielded us from the sun's full wrath. Even so, the temperature must have soared beyond 100 degrees. Sweat began to bead on my brow, snaking down my spine before I'd even taken ten steps toward the entrance.

Near the base of the colossal structure, just steps from the hot, shimmering pavement of the parking lot, I found a small gathering of about twenty people waiting. Most were couples—some elderly, others young and energetic—hailing from nearly every corner of the world. Their languages blended into a soft buzz of excitement and anticipation. I stood alone, the only solo traveler in the bunch, and it wasn't long before cameras were being handed to me with eager smiles. Apparently, solitude makes one the default photographer. I snapped shot after shot of beaming couples posing in front of the towering monument, their bodies silhouetted against the timeless structure.

After a flurry of flashbulbs and polite thank yous, I was relieved when our guide finally arrived. A man in his mid-fifties, he had deeply tanned skin, slick dark hair, and an intensity in his dark eyes that suggested a hair-trigger temper. His commanding voice sliced through the group's chatter. He didn't introduce himself so much as declare his presence.

"Listen up," he barked. "There are rules. Two of them. And you will follow them."

His tone dripped with condescension. I felt like a teenager being scolded by a particularly bitter school principal. Rule one: We were to stay together. No exceptions. Rule two—reinforced with glaring eyes and a pointed finger—was: No one, under any circumstances, was to wander into roped-off areas.

"Do not test me," he said, practically seething. "Severe consequences will follow."

The group fell silent. His passion for these rules was unsettling, and not a single person dared raise a question when he asked for them.

"No questions? Good. Follow me."

We crossed the threshold into the pyramid, and immediately, the oppressive heat gave way to a dense, suffocating coolness. The corridor inside was dimly lit and damp, the stone walls leaching centuries of moisture into the air. The scent was unmistakable—earthy and old, a pungent mixture of stone, sweat, and the heavy breath of time. We walked slowly, single file, between steel hand-rails as we ascended the narrow, sloped passageway of the Grand Gallery.

The deeper we ventured, the heavier the air became. It felt thick, as though the pyramid itself were inhaling, drawing us inward. Sweat that had poured from my body outside now clung to me, unable to evaporate. Yet, despite the oppressive atmosphere, the temperature dropped significantly. It was a welcome relief from the blazing sun.

Eventually, we reached the Queen's Chamber, and the group squeezed in tightly, shoulder-to-shoulder. The space was disappointingly austere—dark, cramped, and eerily silent but for the low murmur of the guide's lecture. From my vantage in the corridor just outside, the chamber's condition struck me: worn walls dulled with time, dingy lighting that looked decades old, and an overall sense of neglect. For a landmark of such renown, it felt ... forgotten.

Rather than join the others in their cramped discomfort, I chose to remain in the corridor, savoring the extra space and solitude. Watching the tourists packed in like sardines, their bodies brushing against one another, made my skin crawl. I turned my gaze away from the crowd and allowed my senses to roam.

As I took in the surroundings, a strange and familiar sensation settled over me. It was like déjà vu—only stronger. The room, the walls, even the faint smell of stone and age—it all seemed intimately familiar. Then, unbidden, a memory surged forth: the Salt Palace. I saw myself being led into a gleaming version of this very chamber by a man in a red silk robe.

A tremor ran through me.

I blinked and looked again. The chamber was no longer just worn; it felt altered. The once pristine walls I remembered from the vision were now scratched and stained. The luminous white granite that had once sparkled under a different kind of light was dulled by time. Something was missing.

I narrowed my eyes, trying to grasp the ghost of the image in my mind. The disparity between what I remembered and what I saw gnawed at me—until, finally, it struck me. The sarcophagus. The beautifully carved, white granite sarcophagus that had stood at the chamber's heart like a sacred centerpiece was gone. Completely vanished. Not even a trace.

Just then, the crowd began to file out, trickling back into the corridor. As the last tourist left the Queen's Chamber, the empty room yawned before me, silent and solemn. My gaze returned to the vacant spot where the sarcophagus should have been. My chest tightened with a mixture of loss and awe.

How had I missed it before?

Sara's voice echoed through my mind, clear and soft like wind over sand:

"You're only at the beginning. To reclaim your full identity, you must undergo training—training that began many lifetimes ago and was interrupted. That's why you're drawn to the mystery schools and their hidden code. You left a message for yourself."

I stood motionless, heart pounding, as past and present began to blur. Somehow, I had been here before. Not in this life—but in another. And the secrets buried beneath stone and silence had only just begun to stir.

The Queen's Chamber had emptied, but I lingered, rooted in place by a gnawing sense that something vital was trying to surface within me. The echo of fading footsteps—my group ascending the steep incline of the Grand Gallery—drew my attention for a moment. I could still hear them, distant and muffled, growing ever fainter as they followed the tour guide toward the King's Chamber. I should have gone with them. I knew that. But I couldn't. Not yet.

I remained still, alone, surrounded by smooth stone walls and centuries of silence. The air was cool here, slightly damp, yet unmoving, as though the pyramid itself were holding its breath. The scent of mineral dust and antiquity filled my lungs. Time stretched. I let the silence settle around me like a shroud.

I closed my eyes. Sara's words from my dreams returned, gentle but commanding: "You must begin your training from where you left off. Only then will you be able to return to your most important past lifetimes. You have left a message for yourself where you will receive your training. Find it, and you will begin to uncover all the answers you seek."

I opened my eyes. The chamber felt different now, as if charged with unseen energy, as if it too were waiting. But waiting for what?

My thoughts scattered as the guide's voice echoed faintly down the stone corridor, a sharp contrast to the stillness around me. He was lecturing the group now about the King's Chamber—its dimensions, its construction, the red granite that lined its walls. My group had arrived. They were learning about the space I was meant to see. And I was still here, lost in questions.

I inhaled deeply and stepped out of the Queen's Chamber. The cool stone pressed beneath my soles as I climbed the rough-hewn steps, ascending slowly through the narrow passage of the Grand Gallery. Shadows danced on the walls, cast by the dim safety lights. Each footstep echoed like a drumbeat in my mind, carrying with it fragments of Sara's messages, half-formed memories, unanswered questions.

When I reached the threshold of the King's Chamber, I paused. The room was packed, shoulder-to-shoulder, a hush falling over the group as the guide droned on. No one noticed I'd been gone. Relief washed over me.

I leaned against the doorway, trying to focus. The guide spoke about the sarcophagus—its material, the same red granite as the chamber. I barely heard him until someone asked, "What about the lid? Wasn't there a lid for the sarcophagus?"

That single question snapped something into focus. It hit me like a strike of lightning. Of course. Every initiatory ritual in my dreams had centered around a sarcophagus—and now here was the last remaining one. The only one left in the world.

The group began to file out, trickling into the hallway behind me, their footsteps receding like a tide pulling back from the shore. Soon, I was alone.

I stepped forward.

The sarcophagus lay at the center of the room, silent and massive. The surface gleamed dully under the low light, its red granite darkened by the ages. It rested exactly where it had been placed millennia ago. My pulse quickened.

Was this it? Was this the purpose of my journey? The object that haunted my dreams, now within arm's reach?

I approached it, heart pounding. Ropes encircled the sarcophagus, a quiet warning. I heard the tour guide's voice in my head: "You will not cross any ropes. The consequences will be severe."

But I was already too far gone.

I waited, frozen, until the pyramid had gone utterly still again. The footsteps of my group had vanished into silence. No sounds, no voices, just the low hum of the ancient walls around me. My fingers trembled. My breath felt shallow.

Now or never.

I stepped over the ropes. My movements were quick, deliberate. I crossed into the restricted space as though I had been meant to do it. My focus narrowed until the rest of the chamber faded away. It was just me and the sarcophagus now.

When I stood before it, I could finally see the missing piece—a massive triangular chunk carved away from the side. I remembered reading about this: the handiwork of vandals, chipping away sacred stone for keepsakes. That theft was the reason this space was now off-limits.

I leaned over the edge and peered inside. To my surprise, I felt ... disappointed. The interior was bare, flat, lined with a thin coat of ancient dust. It was nothing but an empty stone box. Plain. Hollow.

Had I sacrificed everything just to see this?

I tried to shake off the thought. I studied the craftsmanship instead—how had they carved such precision from solid granite with ancient tools? I reminded myself that this box had once meant everything to the mystery schools. And somehow, it still meant everything to me.

No inscriptions. No markings. Just smooth stone. But I felt something pulling me deeper.

I reached out, placing my left hand on the upper edge.

A jolt of energy zipped through me. Not painful, but sharp and sudden—like touching a doorknob after shuffling across a carpet. I froze, stunned.

Then I braced myself again, more cautiously this time. I swung my right foot over the edge and stepped inside.

Dust crunched beneath my foot. I released my hold and swung my left leg over. But as my foot cleared the edge, another surge of electricity shot through me. This one was stronger, intense enough to break my balance.

I staggered.

I wasn't fully inside yet. One foot hovered mid-air, and I swayed like a branch in a high wind. My foot slipped. My hands scrambled for something to grab, but the smooth granite offered no salvation. The dust beneath my feet gave way.

I was falling.

Time slowed.

I saw the fall play out in fragments: my hands flailing, searching, the inevitability of stone rising up to meet me. Thoughts crashed through my mind—panic, regret, disbelief.

Why hadn't I listened?

What had I come here to do?

Then, instinct. I threw my arms behind me, palms wide, grasping for purchase. My fingertips grazed the edge of the sarcophagus' wall. I caught myself.

For a heartbeat, I had hope.

But it was too late. My fingers slipped. And the world went black.

15

When consciousness finally returned, it did so slowly, like mist receding from a damp forest floor. I found myself entombed in an oppressively tight and suffocatingly dark space. The air was thick, stale, and reeked faintly of stone and ancient silence. My limbs were stiff and confined, my head foggy, and I was overwhelmed by an eerie sense of unfamiliarity. Whatever this place was, it wasn't the red quartz granite sarcophagus in the King's Chamber. I had been moved. And I had no idea where.

Panic flared in my chest like fire catching dry brush. My mind raced with wild possibilities, all clawing for dominance. Had I been discovered? Had the guide made good on his warning? The tight enclosure felt like punishment—a sentence carried out in silence and secrecy. If so, the consequences were indeed severe.

Driven by a growing desperation, I reached out into the dark. My fingers trembled as they groped upward, searching for my prison's boundaries. My hand struck something hard and metallic. Cold. Smooth. Heavy. I followed its form from my ribcage up to the top of my head. A dawning horror began to spread through me like ice in water.

I was wearing something.

Something that enveloped my entire upper body.

An ornate mask—golden, intricate. My breath caught. The idea was absurd. It couldn't be real. And yet it was the only thing that made sense. My mind flashed back to the dreams, the visions, and the artifact in the Salt Palace. The golden mask of Tutankhamen—radiant, regal, imprisoning.

A strange blend of disbelief and familiarity wrapped itself around me. My heart pounded like a war drum as I pressed my palms against the smooth interior of the space, feeling the cold, dense stone that surrounded me. I felt as if I had been interred in a tomb.

Fear gripped me like a vise. My breath quickened as I frantically searched the chamber's interior, palms sweeping over stone polished to a flawless, unnerving finish. My fingers searched for a seam, a crack, an imperfection—anything. I found nothing.

Then I remembered: in the King's Chamber, the sarcophagus had once been sealed with a single, impossibly heavy granite lid. Was I beneath such a slab now? Was I meant to suffocate in silence, alone in ancient stone?

I pressed my hands against the ceiling. Reaching it was difficult—I had to stretch my arms nearly to full extension. The awkwardness of my position rendered my legs almost useless. But I had to try.

With a grunt of exertion, I pushed. The slab above me might as well have been a mountain. It did not move. Not even a groan of protest. I tried again, straining every fiber of my being. Nothing. I rested, sweat dripping down my temples, pooling into the folds of the golden mask.

I had read about moments like these—when adrenaline and sheer will could grant impossible strength. People lifting cars to save children. Could I summon that same desperation-fueled power? I saw it in my mind's eye: the slab shifting, light streaming in, freedom.

Again, I pushed. Harder. Longer. My muscles screamed, my vision swam.

Still, nothing.

Time became meaningless. Minutes bled into hours. I repeated the attempt again and again until my arms trembled with fatigue, my body soaked in sweat and despair.

I couldn't do it alone.

And just as that thought coalesced fully in my mind, the silence around me shifted.

Footsteps.

Soft, deliberate, unmistakable. They padded through the chamber just beyond my stone shell. My breath hitched. I froze, heart hammering so loudly I feared it might give me away. Someone was out there.

I pressed my ear to the stone. The footsteps stopped.

Then, a low, grinding rumble.

The stone above me shivered, sending tremors down into the sarcophagus walls. Dust trickled down like powdered bone. My pulse surged.

Light.

A sliver, faint and distant, pierced the darkness above. Fresh air followed—cool, blessed, alive. I gasped as it swept into the enclosure, filling my lungs like salvation. The granite lid continued to move, revealing more of the chamber with each agonizing second.

Above me, the ceiling shimmered with black reflective stone—obsidian-like, perfect. Then, as shadows moved across the widening gap, figures appeared. Hooded. Dark. Silent.

Two approached.

Despite my panic, something in their movement was measured, non-threatening. They stopped just short of the sarcophagus, waiting for the lid to be fully removed. When it was, a dozen more figures came into view—silent sentinels encircling the chamber, their glowing green eyes fixed on me from beneath deep hoods.

I tried to rise, but the mask—I had forgotten the mask. It pressed down on me like a crown forged from lead. I gasped beneath its weight, feeling both trapped and exposed. The figures loomed closer, their bodies radiating heat, their silent presence stifling. I was being smothered by shadows, their eyes burning with alien intelligence.

Panic surged again. My breath caught. I couldn't move. I couldn't escape. My mind screamed.

And then, they began to whisper.

I couldn't understand the language, but the cadence and tone made it clear: They were speaking of me.

Two of the figures leaned in, working together to remove the golden headpiece. Their hands were swift, deliberate. Leather straps loosened. The weight lifted. At once, I could breathe. I surged upright, face-to-face with the man from the Salt Palace—the same olive-skinned stranger with the regal bearing and searching gaze.

His eyes bore into mine, deep and knowing. I felt as if he were peeling back the layers of my soul with a glance. He said nothing for several long seconds. Then he smiled softly.

"Do not be alarmed, Tutankhamen," he said, voice velvet-warm. "Disorientation is expected after what you have just endured."

My mind reeled.

Tutankhamen?

I struggled to answer, to find footing on the crumbling terrain of my reality. "What ... experience are you talking about? Where am I?"

He regarded me curiously, as if I'd asked him to name the sun. "You are in the temple's lower chamber. You have just completed your Dark Night of the Soul."

Dark Night of the Soul.

The words hung in the air like smoke from an ancient fire.

He extended his hand, helping me rise from the sarcophagus. I stood shakily, disoriented and overwhelmed. Around me, the shadowy figures stood still, their gazes unwavering.

"Come," the man said. "Your queen awaits. Let us return to the palace."

As I followed him, one footstep at a time, through the chamber of black stone, I realized the impossible: I was walking inside the world of my dreams, a place shaped by myth, memory, and something more mysterious still. And the journey had only just begun.

16

The moment the hierophant uttered the word "queen," a ripple of anxiety stirred within me. My breath caught ever so slightly. Who was this queen I would soon meet? Every fiber of my being hoped it would be Sara. She had been a constant presence in my dreams of this place, like a radiant thread woven through the fabric of my unconscious mind. But my desires mattered little in this strange world shaped more by destiny than choice. I had to surrender to the current of fate.

As I stepped out of the sarcophagus, the chamber revealed itself in full. Darkness clung to its surfaces like a velvet curtain. A heavy stillness permeated the air, as though the stone itself were holding its breath. Every inch of the chamber, from the smooth, seamless walls to the domed ceiling high above, shimmered with the cool sheen of black granite. The material was polished to such perfection that it mirrored faint reflections of torchlight, like stars glimmering on a night sea.

Moisture hung in the air, thick and chill, and the damp scent of time—old, musty, and rich—filled my nostrils. I could almost taste the centuries in each breath. The hierophant led our group up a narrow staircase carved directly into the rock. Each sandstone step was worn and uneven, as if shaped by countless feet before ours. The shaft's walls pressed in tightly around us, a confining artery leading us upward from the silent tomb of the pit into something wholly unknown.

As we ascended into the Grand Gallery, a transformation occurred. The oppressive underground atmosphere gave way to a broader, more open corridor lined with smooth blocks of golden sandstone. The air shifted—crisper, lighter, with the faint scent of fresh earth and wind. Gone were the metallic railings and weathered stones I remembered from the modern structure. Everything here looked new, pristine—as if the stone itself had just been laid. I was walking not through history, but inside of it.

Then, we reached the gallery's edge. Just twenty feet ahead, sunlight spilled into the corridor like molten gold, casting long, dancing shadows on the floor. As I stepped through the wide opening and out into the world, I gasped.

Gone was the harsh, sunbaked desert I remembered. Before me stretched an emerald paradise. Rolling hills of deep green unfurled across the land like a living tapestry, speckled with wildflowers and towering palms heavy with vines. The air was thick with the scent of blooming jasmine and damp earth. I was reminded of the California wine country, where I had wandered in a different life, under very different skies.

Fifty feet ahead, a broad staircase descended from the pyramid into this verdant valley. At the foot of the stairs stood a gathering of people—colorfully dressed in silks and linens that caught the sun like stained glass. They stood in relaxed conversation, as if awaiting the return of a dear friend.

She was among them.

Sara.

Her face glowed with the soft warmth of familiarity. Her laughter—a sound I would recognize in any lifetime—floated across the distance between us like a song meant only for me. She was surrounded by women, chatting easily, but the moment our eyes met, time fractured.

Emotion rose in me like a tidal wave. Tears welled up, unbidden, and spilled down my cheeks. My heart pounded wildly; my breath caught in my throat. Nothing could have prepared me for this—seeing her again, not in dreams, but in vivid, living color.

And yet I realized with a kind of aching clarity that this wasn't *my* Sara—the one I had loved in a future long yet to come. This was Sara from a different time, a woman who knew me only as Tutankhamen, the young pharaoh. She hadn't shared those memories we would someday create together. Her heart carried love for a man I barely understood, even though I now bore his name, his face.

Still, love knows no boundaries—not of time, not of memory.

As if sensing the storm inside me, Sara turned fully toward me. Her gaze locked with mine. We stood there, suspended in a silent exchange more profound than any spoken language. In her eyes, I saw recognition—not of facts or shared histories, but of souls intertwined beyond lifetimes.

She ran to me.

Her arms flung wide, and I caught her in an embrace that swallowed the world. Our bodies collided with the force of long-lost gravity, and a shock of warm energy surged through me, lighting every nerve. When her lips met mine, the kiss carried all the sorrow of separation and the joy of reunion. It was wordless poetry, a song we both remembered but had forgotten how to sing.

She pulled back and brought her lips to my ear.

"Welcome back, my love. We have been apart for far too long. I feared I might have lost you. But now, I see our bond truly is eternal."

Her words were sunlight through a thunderstorm. I tried to hold back my tears, but they flowed freely, unstoppable. Flashes of our shared lives—distant memories, laughter, whispered secrets, starlit embraces—flared through my mind like constellations returning to their rightful sky.

"You have no idea what I've been through," I choked. "I've dreamed of this moment for so long."

Words failed to convey the crushing weight of years spent mourning, yearning, aching for just this one chance. No expression could fully contain the overwhelming emotion that coursed through me. My soul, once buried beneath grief, had awakened.

The hierophant, Anubis, stood nearby, his face etched with calm curiosity. He waited with respectful silence before signaling it was time to continue. His eyes, though unreadable, held understanding.

"Thank you, Anubis," Sara said softly, "for returning him to me."

We began walking, hand-in-hand. The sandstone path ahead twisted gently through walls of lush green vegetation, the kind of dreamlike jungle one might expect in ancient myths. The air was thick with birdsong and the hum of insects. Water flowed nearby, cool and clear, whispering through channels cut into the earth.

I looked back over my shoulder and gasped.

The Great Pyramid no longer looked like the worn, jagged ruin I remembered. Its stepped surfaces had been restored to a flawless sheen of white limestone, glowing under the sun like a beacon of divine craftsmanship. It radiated purity, dignity, and sacred power—no longer just a monument, but a living shrine.

I recalled from my research that the casing stones had once gleamed like this, long before time and conquest stripped them away to build mosques and mansions. But here, now, the pyramid stood whole. Complete.

We passed laborers tending to emerald fields, surrounded by sheep and goats. Some carried baskets heavy with harvest. Others led oxen through groves and gardens. Each one stopped, bowed, and smiled as we passed. Their reverence was humbling.

Unlike in the future, where machines replaced muscle, here, everything was done by hand. I felt both admiration and pity—admiration for their endurance, pity for their burdens. Still, their faces shone with purpose, even joy. Perhaps, in simplicity, they had preserved something we had lost.

As we crossed a wooden bridge spanning the Nile, I gazed down at the river's surface, where hundreds of fishing boats bobbed gently. Each tiny vessel was filled with men casting nets, their bodies lean and taut from labor. I imagined their thoughts, distant and full of dreams. Were they, too, thinking of the future? Did they also sacrifice the present for what might never come?

I squeezed Sara's hand a little tighter.

In that moment, I vowed not to squander the miracle I had been given. Time had folded itself for us, carved open a sacred space to feel, to love, to *be*. And I would not let it slip away again.

Not now. Not ever.

17

We passed through the massive black-rod iron gates—those same towering bars I'd watched crumble under the weight of an angry mob in my dreams. A hush fell over me as déjà vu washed up again, each step echoing fragments of nightmares come to life. The palace before us was identical in every detail: sandstone walls stretching skyward, round columns ascending in perfect symmetry. It felt impossible, surreal—I kept waiting for the dream to peel away and reveal reality, but the polished stone only confirmed my disbelief.

Inside the gates, the palace crouched along the Nile's western bank. I craned my neck to the second-floor balcony—the one I'd stood on, speaking with Sara, gazing down at the angry crowd scrawled across one of my dreams. Now it lined up perfectly with the rocky riverbanks below, the scene so vividly familiar it made my pulse quicken.

We wound through the grounds, moving beneath high, ivory-hued perimeter walls—walls I'd seen besieged by crowds in shadowed visions. Everywhere I looked, guards stood firm, their bronze armor glinting and their movements taut with readiness. It comforted me, knowing their spears formed a silent promise of protection.

Inside the palace, we received a warm reception—too warm, in fact. My chest tightened under the weight of unsolicited honor. After polite exchanges and delicate courtesies, I was informed of my visitors: Ay, my chief advisor, and General Horemheb, newly returned from a mission in Nubia. Two-thousand elite soldiers had vanished. Now, only the general and a handful of his men remained. Their story, I was told, was urgent.

We entered the dining chamber—a grand hall adorned with tapestries and lit by oil lamps that danced against dark wood. A towering rectangular table, stained like wet mahogany, could seat twenty. I was seated at the head on a throne-like chair, its gilded frame inset with lapis and carnelian. It felt heavy and alien, an object of luxury I'd scarcely ever known.

To my right, Anubis settled into an equally ornate seat. To my left, Sara's calm presence soothed my nerves—still scarlet-tinged with emotion from our reunion. A few chairs down on my right, Ay sat like a coiled serpent. His salt-and-pepper hair, olive skin, and jet-black eyes held arrogant promise. Everything about him felt contrived, venomous. My gut wound tighter.

Across from Ay sat General Horemheb. Younger, imposing even in repose, with cropped hair and a soldier's posture. His face betrayed fatigue and fear. He radiated authenticity—someone who owed nothing to courtly games.

Ay wasted no time. His tone was cutting; he demanded punishment for Horemheb, branding his tale of disappearance as nonsense. "Ludicrous," he spat. "Preposterous." He leveled the general's account with contempt, questioning his integrity.

I watched Ay's chest heave—his fury barely controlled. Anubis, serene, placed a hand on my arm. "Pharaoh

Tutankhamen bears no fault for his father's errors," he said gently. "We must consider this carefully."

I drew a breath. "I'm not interested in conflict." My voice shook, but I pressed forward. "Something grave has happened. General, tell me what occurred in Nubia."

Horemheb's face whitened, his limbs tensing. He glanced at Ay, seeking permission before he spoke. Eventually, he cleared his throat. "We were dispatched to secure gold from miners—again. But this time ... something had changed."

He paused, swallowing. "Their leader confronted us—calm, unwavering. He warned us: 'My god watches us. Do not come.'"

Anubis leaned forward. "How did you respond?"

Horemheb's shoulders dropped. "I laughed. I asked who would enforce his warning with just a god on his side?" The laughter of the soldiers echoed in the vaulted hall.

Anubis's expression remained unreadable—interest beneath his calm. "And his response?"

"He said his god was ready to act—right then." Horemheb's voice trembled as he laid out what came next: two-thousand men, elite soldiers, swept away by an invisible force in an open field. In under five minutes, nearly all were gone—airborne, lifeless, scattered. Only twenty survived.

My spine chilled. Ay's face contorted with rage. "How did you survive—when your men died?" he shouted.

Horemheb swallowed again and answered flatly: "I awoke, days later, in a dark cavern—bound. I don't know where. I could not escape."

Ay banged his fist on the table. "How did you come free?"

"We were…released by him," Horemheb said softly.

Ay scoffed. "By whom? An invisible phantom?"

Horemheb fixed Ay with a steady gaze. "He appeared as Sekhmet…but called himself Drunvalo. I know what I saw. He said if we came again—he would come to Egypt."

Ay sprang from his seat, pointing at Horemheb. "This is blasphemy! We must march our armies now—against this imposter god!"

Anubis raised a placating hand. "Not so fast." He paused, meeting Ay's glare. "Tutankhamen … these aren't simple human forces we're dealing with."

He explained the legends—the Atlanteans, the progenitors of our civilization, worshiped as gods. Sekhmet might be one of them. Ay's sneer didn't falter. Legend, he scoffed. Nonsense.

Anubis pressed on, calm but firm: "Drunvalo's ability to fling two-thousand warriors—his god-status—these fit the myths."

Ay turned to me, expectant, quivering with menace. Silent, I recognized my moment. I raised my voice above the tension: "We won't rush into war. We will learn. We will investigate this Drunvalo—before we strike."

A weight lifted in the room. Ay's chest heaved with rage unspent; others breathed, relieved. I felt the hall's atmosphere shift—ancient stones exhaling tension and opening to a new direction.

In that hush, I realized something profound had stirred—unseen but unstoppable. And I, Pharaoh Tutankhamen, must walk the balance between mortal politics and unfathomable power.

18

Once our discussion ended, the group filed solemnly out of the dining hall. Ay and the general were quietly escorted through the gilded entryway and toward the outer palace grounds, their footsteps echoing faintly behind them. Meanwhile, Anubis, Ankehesenpaaten, and I turned down another corridor, our sandals brushing softly against the polished stone floor as we wandered deeper into the heart of the royal residence.

Room after room unfurled before us like a living gallery of art and elegance. Every space within the palace radiated opulence. The walls shimmered with a muted glow from the torches, their flames flickering gently against slabs of rich, honey-brown sandstone, carved delicately with mythic scenes and sacred symbols. Golden fixtures—sun disks, falcons, and lotus flowers—adorned every corner, their metallic sheen catching the light like drops of sunlight preserved in metal.

Lavishly carved furnishings surrounded us, each a testament to the era's craftsmanship. Ornate chairs, their deep wood stained to a near-ebony hue, were inlaid with slivers of ivory and gilded hieroglyphs. Cabinets and ceremonial tables bore complex, swirling patterns edged in gold, and the occasional glint of inset gemstones—lapis, carnelian, and turquoise—offered bursts of divine color.

The walls were lined with ceremonial masks, dozens of them, resting silently like vigilant guardians. Their features were both fierce and serene, their eyes rimmed with sapphire and onyx. Embedded jewels—emeralds the size of olives, rubies as deep as coals, and brilliant-cut diamonds like frozen stars—sparkled within them, imbuing the space with a quiet magic. They reminded me of the mask I had worn during the temple rite. The sight of them stirred something ancient within me.

Anubis had remained close, walking silently, always a step behind. His gaze was steady, curious—measuring. I could feel his attention settle on me with a weight I could neither ignore nor fully interpret. Something within me had shifted, and he knew it. I sensed he had known from the moment we'd first locked eyes in the temple. Whatever he saw in me, it did not align with the Tutankhamen he remembered.

We eventually reached a winding staircase spiraling upward toward the palace's upper chambers. But before I could begin the ascent, Anubis gently placed a hand on my arm and gestured to a small door beneath the staircase.

The room beyond was intimate, a private study bathed in soft amber light. Its walls were paneled with pale wood, smooth and fragrant, decorated with flowing murals and tiny metallic sculptures that shimmered like captured moonlight. A dark, lustrous desk stood at the center, its matching chairs carved with sacred symbols and lined with fine linen.

Without a word, Anubis motioned for me to sit. I obeyed, lowering myself into the seat opposite him. He remained standing for a moment, silent, as though allowing the air to settle. Then he took his place across from me, folded his hands on the table, and stared deeply into my eyes.

That gaze—unyielding, ancient—met mine with a force I could only describe as soul-piercing. I felt exposed beneath it, as if my every memory, every secret, was open to his inspection. Did he possess some otherworldly sight? Was he peering through the veil, past my borrowed form, into the essence of who I truly was?

Time seemed suspended as we sat in silence. My heart thudded quietly against my ribs. I didn't know if he was searching for something or waiting for me to break. My mind spun with possibilities. Could he see John Fullman beneath the surface of Tutankhamen's youthful features? Did he know I was not who I appeared to be?

Finally, he broke the silence.

"Tutankhamen," he said softly, his voice low and resonant, "since the completion of your last exercise, I have noticed a change in you. You seem—untethered. Lost, perhaps. When you first encountered Ankhesenpaaten, I feared you were suffering an emotional collapse. Are you well?"

His concern, quiet and genuine, cut through my anxiety like warm light through mist. It disarmed me. His words carried no judgment, only compassion and watchfulness. I exhaled, tension draining from my shoulders.

"I'm all right," I said, carefully. "I've been disoriented, yes. But things are beginning to come into focus now."

Anubis studied me a moment longer. The tightness in his posture eased, and a subtle shift softened his expression. He reached out and placed a warm, steady hand on my shoulder.

"Do you have any questions about what you experienced during the exercise?" he asked.

I paused. My mind raced for a plausible answer. I had no recollection of what Tutankhamen had seen or endured. How could I speak to an experience I had never lived?

"No," I said finally. "I think I understand."

He withdrew his hand, his brow furrowed with subtle surprise. He leaned back slightly, studying me again. Perhaps he had expected more engagement, or more curiosity. Or perhaps he already suspected the truth.

"Most initiates struggle to interpret what they see beyond the body," he said slowly. "When your deepest fears manifest into tangible forms, it is not to torment you, but to free you. These trials reveal your eternal self."

His words resonated with something deep within me. I couldn't respond. I could only listen.

"The essence of who you are exists beyond the material world. It is untouched by time, by harm, by suffering. When you fully realize this, you understand that nothing in the physical world can truly harm you. The pain you feel only holds power if you choose to identify with it."

He leaned in, his voice low and reverent.

"Your true power lies in your awareness of this eternal self. You were created from the same energy as the stars, the rivers, and the great void that gave birth to the universe. You carry the same potential. Every action you take, every thought you hold, shapes the fabric of this world."

I remained quiet, struck by the clarity and depth of his words. They reached me—not only as Tutankhamen, but as John Fullman. Somehow, I knew what he was saying was true.

Anubis stood and walked to the door. As he opened it, he turned once more.

"I will let you rest now. I wanted you to hear these truths before your next trial begins."

And with that, he vanished into the corridor, leaving me with the silence, and with a heart heavy with questions.

I sat for a long moment, digesting his words. Questions about the mystery schools, the temples, the meaning of all I had experienced buzzed in my mind. But I held them back. There would be time.

Eventually, I rose and stepped out into the corridor. The heavy wooden door creaked shut behind me as I looked around, hoping to find Sara. I searched the lower level to no avail, only to learn from the guards that she had gone up to the royal chambers.

Doing my best to appear confident, I ascended the grand staircase, though the palace's layout was still unfamiliar. I couldn't shake the feeling that I was moving through a dream.

And yet I was slowly beginning to accept the impossible truth: I had once lived as Tutankhamen. I had walked these halls before. I had been a student of the mysteries. But how had I returned to this place, to this time? Was it the sarcophagus? Did it hold some hidden power? Was it a portal?

The thought brought to mind the inexplicable pull I had always felt toward the Great Pyramid. Even as a child, its image had stirred something deep and old within me—a memory, perhaps, buried beneath layers of forgotten time.

As I neared the royal chamber, I thought again of Sara. Our connection had always been profound, but now it felt eternal. Could souls travel through lifetimes together? Had we always been bound this way?

I remembered the first time I had seen her, two decades ago. One look had shattered every emotional defense I had ever built. Her eyes had seen through me, as if she had known me for centuries. Perhaps she had.

I began to wonder about the nature of all my most meaningful relationships. Were we a constellation of souls, returning again and again, guiding each other toward deeper growth? Were our lives choreographed not by chance, but by necessity?

Even though each new lifetime wipes clean the slate of memory, perhaps something deeper remains. Perhaps beneath the surface, those eternal bonds persist.

And maybe that's why, when we meet those who are truly meant for us, we *know*. Not with the mind, but with the soul.

Some connections defy logic. They aren't formed—they are remembered.

And I was just beginning to remember everything.

19

I entered the royal chamber with a single, unshakable thought echoing through my mind: Sara was quite possibly the most important person in my world. Despite the times she had challenged me, even exasperated me with her complexity, I was beginning to understand that perhaps everything she brought to the surface in those moments was exactly what I needed. She was my mirror, my catalyst, my key to growth. Maybe her fire wasn't meant to burn me, but to illuminate the parts of myself I had yet to fully face.

The chamber itself was bathed in a golden hush, the kind of light that feels sacred, as if borrowed from the gods. I stepped deeper into its ancient stillness, my breath catching slightly at the beauty that unfolded before me. There, just beyond the open doors to the balcony, Ankehesenpaaten was reclined gracefully on a vividly patterned sofa, its cushions woven in rich crimsons, sapphire blues, and sun-warmed golds. She looked utterly serene, draped in flowing linen that caught the breeze like sails on the Nile.

She was staring out over the lush, green expanse of the west bank, where palm trees swayed gently and the Nile shimmered like liquid silver in the waning afternoon light. Her long, obsidian hair billowed around her shoulders, revealing the delicate curvature of her neckline, the bronze hue of her skin glowing like polished amber. The sight of her stole my breath.

But it was more than beauty that overwhelmed me.

It was her radiance.

There was something I had forgotten—or perhaps had never fully recognized. Sara carried within her a powerful, inner light. It wasn't something seen with the eyes alone, but felt deeply. It permeated the atmosphere around her, shifting it, softening it. Her presence was a force of nature, a quiet miracle that changed everything.

I stood there, suspended in awe, suddenly aware that I might not have fully understood the gift I was being offered by her. I had longed for this moment—had begged the universe for another chance. Now that it was here, I feared I wasn't entirely worthy of it. Had I truly been seeing her? Or had I only been seeing what I expected, what I projected, what I feared?

She hadn't yet turned around. She didn't need to.

Her presence called to me like gravity.

As I stepped closer, lost in the reverie of her silhouette against the horizon, I didn't realize she had already sensed me. When she turned her head slightly and caught my eyes, time unraveled. Her smile was warm, knowing. Her eyes, dark and fathomless, pierced through every defense I'd ever built. Every emotion I'd buried surged to the surface.

I reached out to her, and she stood to meet me. Without a word, we embraced.

The moment she wrapped her arms around me, I broke. Tears I hadn't known I'd been holding in streamed down my face. My entire body shuddered in her arms as a dam within me collapsed. Grief, longing, gratitude, and a love so immense it bordered on pain—it all flooded through me. She held me tighter, whispering soft, wordless sounds into my ear as if cradling a wounded animal.

We had found each other again.

In that embrace, I felt her soul merge with mine. A current of warm electricity surged through our bodies, a tingling wave that fused us together beyond flesh. We held on, tighter and tighter, neither of us willing to loosen our grip for fear the moment might vanish like smoke. Her lips found mine, and the kiss we shared wasn't passion—it was remembrance. It was eternity folding into a single instant.

When she finally spoke, her voice was delicate but steady.

"I have never seen you so overwhelmed with emotion. Please tell me why you are suffering. Does it have something to do with your recent experience in the temple?"

I pulled back slightly, brushing a tear from her cheek, and nodded.

"In the temple," I said, struggling to find words for a pain beyond language, "I experienced my greatest fear. I lost you. You were gone, and I was left in a world without you. It was hollow. Pointless. I didn't want to go on."

At that, her own tears began to fall—soft rivers tracing the contours of her face. She pressed her forehead against mine and whispered, "Oh, my love," before pulling me back into another kiss, deeper this time. Her lips were warm and trembling, tasting of tears and truth.

And then she said it, the words I hadn't even known I needed:

"I will always be with you. Our souls are eternally bound. Even when we part in this life, we are never truly apart. Love like ours cannot die. It is the thread that weaves through every lifetime. And whenever you feel lost, you need only close your eyes and remember."

I wept again.

Perhaps she was right.

Perhaps the Universe wasn't cruel for separating us. Perhaps it was kind for allowing us to find one another again.

"Ankhesenpaaten," I said, my voice raw with emotion, "if I've never said this before, I'm so sorry. I love you more than life itself. You are my everything. Losing you nearly destroyed me. But I see it now. I see you. And I swear I will never take your presence for granted again."

She rested her head against my chest, and we stayed that way until the sun slipped behind the Great Pyramid in the distance, leaving a sky of molten gold and indigo in its wake.

We lay together on the couch outside, wrapped in one another. The wind grew cooler, rustling the date palms. The sky deepened to velvet. Stars blinked into view, quiet witnesses to our reunion.

In that moment, I had everything I needed.

Still, I couldn't help but feel the quiet ache of impending loss. The irony of it all was devastating. I had traveled into my past to heal the wound of losing her in my future. But even as I was being made whole again, I knew Ankehesenpaaten stood on the edge of her own heartbreak. She would soon lose me.

I could only hope that her faith in the teachings of the mystery schools—her unwavering belief in the eternal soul—would carry her through the storm.

Because I had been to that abyss.

And I had barely survived it.

As night fell fully and the desert sky turned black, I held her closer, memorizing the weight of her in my arms, the sound of her breath, the rhythm of her heartbeat. I never wanted to let go. But in the deepest part of me, I knew...

I would have to.

20

Just to the south of the Pharaoh's great palace, nestled along the golden curve of the Nile's west bank, stood a fortified compound shrouded in both wealth and secrecy. This was the opulent domain of Ay, a man of ambition, cunning, and dark intent. The late afternoon sun scorched the valley with waves of heat that shimmered against the sand, but inside the lavish throne room of Ay's palace, another kind of heat simmered—one born of rising tempers and veiled threats.

The room was an extravagant gallery of plundered beauty. Imported tapestries from Phoenicia draped the high stone walls, their woven golden threads glinting dimly in the filtered light. Columns carved from alabaster and obsidian soared toward a painted ceiling depicting ancient battles and divine coronations. Every object in sight was a statement of power—golden thrones, inlaid tables of cedar and ivory, and obsidian chalices rimmed in silver. But none of this opulence could cool the fire building between Ay and the iron-jawed General Horemheb.

Though the two men were shielded from the desert's oppressive sun, their discussion burned hotter with each exchanged word. Ay stood rigid near the throne, his sharp eyes blazing with frustration. Horemheb, equally tall but more grizzled from years of war, braced himself against a column, arms crossed, his gaze unmoving.

"Enough excuses," Ay snapped, his voice slicing through the still air like a bronze blade. "I trusted you to deliver Nubian gold, and you returned with empty hands and tales of mythical warriors."

Horemheb remained stone-faced, but the tension in his jaw betrayed him. "The man we faced wasn't a myth, Ay. Drunvalo fights like no mortal I've seen. Even my Immortals couldn't touch him. He fights like a god—if not Sekhmet herself reborn."

Ay scoffed. He turned away and paced slowly beneath a towering statue of Amun-Ra. The flickering torchlight made his silhouette ripple with menace.

"I have spent my life in the shadows of unworthy rulers," he growled. "I was the architect behind Egypt's stability, the hand behind every great decision. And now? I'm to sit idly while a boy-king chases mystic fantasies? No. This throne was meant for me."

He spun on his heel and fixed his gaze on Horemheb.

"Tutankhamen is weak. Obsessed with temples and dreams while the empire rots at its edges. The people need a ruler—not a dreamer. If Drunvalo brings chaos to our borders, we crush him. You will return to Nubia with the remainder of our forces."

Horemheb's throat tightened. He had faced death before, but this mission felt different. It felt like a trap not only for him, but for Egypt itself.

"Our troops are weary," he said, voice steady but tinged with caution. "And Drunvalo … he won't stop. If we provoke him again, I fear what he might do. To us. To the Pharaoh."

Ay's eyes narrowed, and his tone dropped to a cold, predatory whisper.

"Let him. That is precisely the point. Let him rise. Let him strike. And then we will bury him under the weight of our empire."

Then, with venom sharpening every syllable, he added, "Or perhaps he will do what I cannot. Perhaps he will rid us of the boy-king altogether."

The words hung in the air, heavy and poisonous.

Horemheb blinked. A deadly silence stretched between them.

Ay stepped closer, his face now inches from the general's. His voice turned to iron.

"You will obey me. Or I will extinguish every last ember of your bloodline. Not just your wife. Not just your children. I will find your cousins in the oasis towns. Your sisters in Memphis. Your aging uncles on the Delta. And I will make them scream."

Horemheb felt the air drain from the room. He had always known Ay was ruthless. But this—this was madness stitched in gold.

There was no choice. Resistance would mean death for everyone he held dear.

Swallowing his pride, Horemheb bowed his head.

"How will I move the army without Tutankhamen discovering?" he asked, his voice subdued.

Ay's rage abated slightly, satisfied with the general's submission. He gestured toward the darkening horizon outside the narrow window.

"In three days' time, the boy will be sealed inside the sarcophagus chamber for his initiation. He will be deaf to the world. Blind to our actions. Move then."

The general nodded, though his eyes remained clouded with unease.

"Drunvalo warned me. He said there would be no mercy if I returned."

Ay turned away, arms crossed behind his back as he stared into the flickering shadows.

"Then return with fury," he said softly. "Or return not at all."

The torchlight flickered as if recoiling from the weight of his words. The palace fell into silence again, save for the low hiss of oil flames and the distant roar of the Nile.

And in that silence, one truth remained: Egypt teetered on the edge of betrayal, and the gods themselves seemed to hold their breath.

21

The sun had only just risen, but already its relentless blaze bore down upon us with the weight of a thousand fires. Each golden ray, sharp and unwavering, lanced through the thin morning air, searing our skin and filling the sky with a blinding brilliance. We walked in a solemn procession behind Anubis and his twelve priests, the rhythmic shuffle of our feet muted beneath the grandeur of the desert's silence. Our ceremonial robes shimmered like water in the heat, their delicate silk threads catching the light in dazzling flashes. Hues of pale ivory, pearl, and gold rippled with each movement, painting a living mosaic of reverence and ritual.

As we approached the Great Pyramid, the world seemed to shift. The sun's angle crowned the priests in radiant halos; their ashen-white garments blazed with a divine intensity that made it nearly impossible to look directly at them. And yet my gaze was irresistibly drawn to Anubis. He walked several paces ahead, his stride fluid and deliberate, like a man accustomed to commanding more than just attention. He wore a crimson robe that smoldered beneath the sunlight, and a golden crown encrusted with gleaming stones rested atop his head, catching fire with every step. In his right hand, he carried an ivory staff, polished to a mirror sheen and inscribed with ancient glyphs that seemed to pulse with latent power.

But it wasn't his attire that captivated me—it was something deeper, something intangible. He seemed to radiate an energy that warped the very fabric of space around him. The air shimmered more vividly in his presence. Colors grew more vibrant, and shadows receded as though they, too, acknowledged his light. Where Anubis walked, the world transformed. There was a sacred weight in his being, as if he carried the essence of stars within his soul.

Following him was like stepping through a dream. I felt weightless and grounded all at once, my senses alight with awe. Every leaf, every breeze, every shimmer of light seemed amplified, wrapped in a silent harmony that transcended understanding. I couldn't help but wonder if he had somehow alchemized his own spirit, infusing the physical world with something of himself. Was this transformation merely perception, or had he truly altered the nature of reality around him?

Beside me, Ankehesenpaaten moved in quiet grace, her presence a balm against the intensity of the moment. We exchanged few words, both lost in the vivid procession of light and color around us. Her eyes, serene and knowing, occasionally met mine, grounding me when the spectacle threatened to sweep me away.

The sun reached its zenith just as we stood before the pyramid's yawning entrance. With one final glance at the sky, I stepped into the shadow. The shift was immediate and profound. Coolness enveloped us, wrapping around our heated skin like a blessing. A collective breath was exhaled by our group, relief washing over our faces.

Inside, the Grand Gallery loomed, its high ceiling and ascending passage creating a corridor of solemn mystery.

Our steps echoed against stone worn by the centuries, and as we ascended the uneven sandstone steps, my heart began to thump with nervous anticipation. I clutched Ankehesenpaaten's hand tighter. She responded without words, her touch full of quiet strength.

We reached the Queen's Chamber, and the moment I crossed its threshold, I was overcome with awe. It was just as it had appeared in my dreams—a chamber bathed in ethereal light, its walls, ceiling, and floor crafted from polished white granite that gleamed like starlight. The air hummed with a soft vibration, a resonance that seemed to seep into my bones. Light flooded the room not from any window or torch, but from mysterious white stones that lined the walls, affixed in golden brackets, each casting a pure beam that danced through the space.

In the center of the chamber sat a sarcophagus, carved from the same luminous granite, gleaming like a holy relic. Behind it, wooden tables bore a strange array of objects—metallic, crystalline, and dazzling in their alien intricacy. But it was the large wooden box near the far wall that stopped my breath. Nestled within, the golden mask of Tutankhamen stared back at me, its eyes hollow yet brimming with hidden meaning. My stomach churned. This was no ordinary mask—it was a relic of destiny.

While I stared, the priests moved swiftly and silently. The glowing stones were unboxed and installed. The granite slab was repositioned with uncanny ease. This was not merely preparation—it was choreography, an ancient dance practiced across millennia.

Anubis beckoned me forward. My feet felt heavy, as if weighted by the enormity of what awaited. I let go of Ankehesenpaaten's hand, reluctant to part from her comfort. Two priests guided me to the sarcophagus and began preparing me for the ritual. Around me, the others began to form a sacred circle, their eyes closed in reverence.

I lay down, the stone beneath me surprisingly warm, as if it pulsed with the memory of the sun. From the corner of my eye, I saw two priests approaching, carrying the golden mask. Its radiance was blinding. My breath caught, heart pounding. I remembered the Salt Palace. The visions. The collapse. Fear surged through me.

Panic clawed its way into my chest. I sat up, ready to flee, every cell in my body screaming for escape. The air thickened, and doubt clouded my thoughts. But then—I saw her: Ankhesenpaaten. She stood just beyond the edge of the circle, her gaze locked onto mine. Her eyes, ancient and endless, reached into my soul. In them, I saw home.

She stepped forward, her voice a melody that wrapped around my panic like silk. "Do not be afraid, my love. The exercise you are about to perform will not only benefit you; it will also have a positive impact on your people. Your actions in this moment will affect this world for centuries to come."

I had heard these words before—within the dream, within the Salt Palace. Her presence grounded me, tethered me to something unshakable. I exhaled, slowly lowering myself back into place.

The golden mask descended over my face, plunging me into a world of gold and shadow. Then, the voice of Anubis spoke—not aloud, but within. It was a voice of gravity and warmth, resonating in my mind like the echo of creation itself.

"Tutankhamen," he intoned, "this exercise is to help you find harmony—not in escape from experience, but in complete embrace of its dual nature. Light and shadow, joy and fear, the spiritual and the physical—these are not enemies, but complements. The universe is duality in motion. Your task is not to resist, but to balance.

"You may be tempted to reject the dark, for it wounded you. But in doing so, you deny the full truth of existence. The shadow teaches. The shadow refines. Accept it, walk with it, and you will become whole.

"Detach from the need to label. Become the witness, not the warrior. Let each moment pass through you like wind through reeds. There is power in this surrender, strength in this openness. Do not resist. Observe. Accept. Grow."

His words echoed in a rhythm that seemed to blend with my heartbeat. The world receded, and I drifted into the vastness within myself. The ritual had begun.

And so, lying beneath the weight of gold and prophecy, I surrendered to the mystery. To the light. To the dark. To the eternal truth that everything—every moment, every breath, every fear—was conspiring not to harm me, but to set me free.

I closed my eyes and began to do as Anubis had instructed. Drawing in a slow, deliberate breath, I focused entirely on the rise and fall of my abdomen. Each inhale swelled my stomach gently, and each exhale released the tension coiled deep within me. As my focus narrowed to this simple, primal rhythm, the nervous tremors in my chest began to subside, and the cacophony of anxious thoughts dissolved into silence.

Moments later, Anubis's voice returned, low and resonant, like the echo of wisdom carved into the stones of
time. "That's it. Remember, no matter what occurs, accept
what is given to you in the moment. Let go of resistance.
Immense power lies in surrendering your personal will to
the flow of the universe. My thoughts remain with you."

His words lingered as he rose and stepped away, his
presence retreating like a shadow into the periphery.
Then four solemn priests emerged, moving as one, bearing the weighty slab of white granite. Their faces were
etched with reverence and focus. I watched them place
it upon the sarcophagus with a thunderous finality that
seemed to silence the world.

In that instant, all airflow vanished. The walls closed
in. My breath, which had been the anchor of my calm,
faltered. A wave of claustrophobia surged up from the
pit of my stomach. But instead of succumbing to fear, I
returned to my breath, deeper now, more intentional.
As I refocused, the green gems within the golden mask
began to glow brighter, intensifying like living embers.

The world outside slipped away. Time unspooled. I
was floating between moments, no longer anchored to
breath or body. I don't know how long I lingered in that
suspended state. Consciousness may have left me entirely,
or perhaps I simply melted into the fabric of another
realm.

Then it began.

A sudden explosion of sound ruptured the void, as if
the earth itself cried out. Vibrations rolled through the
sarcophagus like thunder in stone, each wave hammering into my bones. At first, the pulses came slowly, with
enough space between them to catch my breath—but

soon they grew in frequency, cascading one upon another until they became a relentless tide.

Somehow, amid the mounting chaos, I could sense a rhythm hidden within the madness—a subtle pulse, as ancient and deliberate as the beating heart of the cosmos.

My body responded.

My heartbeat quickened, rising to meet the tempo of the sound. My breath shortened, aligning with the pattern that surged through me. I was no longer a passive observer. I was being drawn in, pulled into synchrony with the vibration that surrounded me.

Then, as if summoned by the rhythm, a scent filled the air—rich, sharp, and sacred. It was the unmistakable perfume of burning incense, both sweet and metallic. The air inside the sarcophagus thickened with smoke, swirling in graceful tendrils that clung to my skin. Panic sparked. I struggled to breathe, convinced the smoke would suffocate me.

The emerald light from the gems burned hotter, searing against my face. What had once been soothing was now intolerable. The mask blazed like a furnace, its hundreds of tiny beams piercing into me like focused sunlight through crystal. My skin screamed beneath the invisible fire.

And then came the pain.

A blinding surge of energy tore through me, starting at the crown of my head and cascading down my spine like lightning. My body convulsed, seized by waves of agony that crackled outward into my limbs. The pain was alive, intelligent, unrelenting. It had a will of its own, and it had come to dismantle me.

Time disintegrated. The world shrank to that single, unbearable moment. I was trapped in a loop of pure torment, with no sense of beginning or end. I couldn't breathe. My heart raced to an impossible pace, keeping time with the infernal rhythm echoing all around me.

Then, the tempo shifted again. Faster. Louder. More intense.

My heart tried desperately to keep up. Pain knifed through my chest. I felt a surge of electricity erupt, tearing through every fiber of my being. My limbs spasmed and fell limp, paralyzed. My fingers refused to move. My body was no longer mine.

I was dying.

The realization descended like a final curtain. I could feel my life ebbing away, the last flickers of control slipping through my grasp. And yet, even in that moment, a whisper of clarity came through the storm.

I understood.

The lesson wasn't in resistance. It was in surrender. This suffering wasn't meant to punish me—it was meant to unmake me. To strip away the false identities I clung to. The fear. The pride. The illusion of control.

And just as the darkness reached out to claim me, Anubis's voice echoed through the void, calm and eternal:

"You must learn to separate your identity from your experience. Great power becomes yours when you surrender your will and trust in the order of the universe."

And with those final words, my vision dissolved.

The world went black.

A gentle wind stirred across my face, waking me from the void. As I opened my eyes, the world unfolded in breathtaking strangeness: I was soaring, weightless, suspended high above a vast and shimmering expanse of water. The ocean stretched endlessly below me, a mirror to the heavens, its surface catching the golden hues of the rising sun in rippling ribbons of fire and gold. There were no wings, no machine—just me, flying as if borne aloft by sheer will or some ancient magic.

The air rushed past me in exhilarating gusts, caressing my skin and whipping through my hair, and I was overcome by the sheer mystery of it all. I had no control over my movement, no sense of direction, and no idea where I was being taken. My body hurtled through the sky with astonishing speed, the wind howling in my ears. The sensation was both freeing and terrifying, like a dream balanced on the edge of awe and helplessness.

Far ahead, a thin smudge of land emerged on the horizon, growing rapidly closer. As the distance closed, a sweeping view of a colossal island revealed itself beneath me. I stared, wide-eyed, as the impossible came into focus. This place, lush and tropical, teemed with beauty and order. Nestled among tall palm trees and glowing green foliage was a metropolis that shimmered like a jewel—a city seemingly pulled from myth.

A thousand glinting skyscrapers rose from the earth like polished obelisks, their mirrored surfaces reflecting a sky lit with golden light. It looked like a vision from some far-flung future, a harmony of elegance and advancement. But at the city's heart stood a wonder that stole my breath: an enormous white granite pyramid, its peak crowned in gleaming gold. It dwarfed the Great Pyramid, majestic and ancient, as if it had stood since the dawn of time.

I was spiraling down toward this centerpiece, this radiant monolith, and just before reaching its apex, everything shifted. My awareness twisted, and in an instant, I was no longer just a drifting observer—I had become someone else. Or rather, someone I had once been.

I was seated on a throne of gold, draped in rich crimson silk that shimmered with the energy of sacred power. My hand curled around an ivory staff, identical to the one Anubis carried. Before me, a circle of twelve priests in flowing white robes chanted in unison, their voices resonant and entrancing. The name they spoke—"Drunvalo"—rolled through the chamber like a sacred drumbeat, echoed by the rhythm of deep drums pounding in time with their chant.

Each priest wore a trance-like expression, their faces lit by the glow of unseen energies. Among them, I saw Anubis. The sight of him in this distant time struck me with wonder, but before I could make sense of it, I was pulled away again.

This time, I soared above a vast, mountainous jungle. The terrain below was rugged and cloaked in layers of vibrant green. The thick vegetation glistened with moisture, steaming under the heat of a sun hidden behind drifting clouds. In the distance, I spotted a towering structure: a flat-topped pyramid sitting like a crown atop the tallest peak. Its stone face was worn but powerful, a temple of earth and sky.

Without warning, I was again merged into another past self. I stood among a procession of robed figures, each of us dressed in solemn black, our faces heavy with confusion and fatigue. We moved slowly up the pyramid's steep stone steps, a sluggish, somber march toward something none of us understood.

My body felt foreign, leaden and slow. My thoughts came only in fragments. I knew something was wrong. We were being led like sheep to a place we should have fled from, and yet my feet obeyed the rhythm of the line.

As we neared the summit, a dreadful presence awaited. I made eye contact with a man cloaked in darkness. His eyes were deep voids, and they pierced me with a gaze that froze my blood. My breath caught. I knew this man—not just from this life, but from across time. His presence exuded malice. A sadistic grin crept across his face, feeding off my fear.

The man three places ahead of me screamed as two enormous guards seized him. They dragged him forward to the altar where the dark figure stood waiting. The sinister man's laughter echoed across the rooftop as the poor soul struggled helplessly.

Panic surged through me. I turned, desperate to escape—and locked eyes with Anubis again. He was behind me in the procession, his face blank, as if under a spell. My heart sank. He couldn't save me. He couldn't even save himself.

The line advanced. I was next.

When I tried to flee, powerful arms clamped down on me. I thrashed, kicked, and screamed, but it was useless. They dragged me to the cold altar, its surface stained and scarred from countless sacrifices before mine. Leather straps were lashed around my wrists, pinning me down, stretched and exposed.

The dark priest stepped forward. His face was now close, and I recognized him fully.

Ay.

My advisor. My betrayer.

From within his robe, he drew a gleaming golden dagger. It caught the sunlight and flashed in my eyes, a deadly beam of finality. With no hesitation, he raised the blade high, then drove it down. The impact was searing, a blinding white pain that surged through my chest, exploding outward like a detonation.

Darkness fell.

The world vanished.

And I was gone.

Once more, I soared effortlessly through the air, the wind slicing past me in crisp, invigorating bursts. Below, an entirely new continent unfolded—a land of towering pine forests and steep mountain peaks that seemed to pierce the heavens themselves. The landscape was a stark contrast to the lush, humid jungles I had just departed. This place was one of clarity, of crispness, of alpine majesty.

A dense canopy of shaggy, emerald-green pines blanketed the slopes like an ancient, protective shroud. The mountains stretched endlessly into the distance, their snow-capped peaks glowing under the soft caress of a golden, early morning sun. The tips of these mountains disappeared into thick, swirling banks of clouds, where the air was thin and the sky shimmered a pale silver-blue.

As I glided lower, a singular structure gradually revealed itself—hidden in plain sight, nestled against the shoulder of a great peak. A massive white pyramid, carved from luminous limestone, stood silently beneath the towering cliffs. At first, it was nearly invisible, camouflaged against the snowy canvas of the mountain backdrop. It radiated a stillness so profound it seemed part of the mountain itself, as though it had risen from the earth at the dawn of time.

The pyramid's base was fronted by a wide stone staircase, its tawny-hued steps snaking up the hillside like a river of sculpted earth. These steps were not rigid or manmade in appearance but flowed with the land's natural curvature—twisting and winding organically through clusters of wild azalea, alpine moss, and flowering brush. The stone was warm underfoot and worn smooth by centuries of reverent passage.

Without warning, I was no longer flying. My feet touched the steps, breath laboring slightly in the cool mountain air as I climbed alongside a silent procession of orange-robed monks. Their heads were clean-shaven, their faces calm and composed. I glanced at my own robe, the same radiant orange hue draping over my shoulders. Somehow, I knew I was one of them. A brother. A seeker. A student.

With each step, the energy shifted. The air grew denser with intention, charged with an invisible current that tingled against my skin. A profound sense of reverence welled up inside me—this was sacred ground. As we reached the summit, we stepped into the pyramid's inner sanctum, and a soft, golden light enveloped us.

The pyramid's interior was sublime in its simplicity. Polished white limestone walls glowed gently in the light that filtered down from a narrow shaft in the ceiling, illuminating a circular meditation hall. The scent of sandalwood and blooming herbs drifted through the air, and a soft humming—like the gentle resonance of distant bells—rippled throughout the chamber.

Rows of monks sat in the lotus position on vibrant silk cushions of crimson, saffron, and deep blue. Their eyes were closed, their faces serene. Their chests rose and fell in unison, breathing in the temple's sacred air, breathing out any trace of worldly distraction. The harmony of their energy was palpable. It felt like the very walls of the pyramid were humming in tune with the monks' silent devotion.

I followed the line to an open cushion near the front, settling into place and folding my legs beneath me. The moment I sat down, a wave of tranquility surged through me, settling deep into my bones. The stillness here was not empty—it was full, alive, vast. A silence so complete it sang.

Then I saw him. At the front of the room, guiding the group with nothing but the depth of his breath and the resonance of his presence, stood the master. Tall, draped in a robe of crimson silk that shimmered like liquid flame, his hands rested lightly in his lap; his posture was regal and perfectly still.

Anubis.

His gaze met mine, and time ceased to exist. In that single moment, I felt everything—joy, peace, belonging. Such eternal recognition stretches across lifetimes and echoes through the soul like the remembered note of a long-forgotten song. His eyes were deep wells of wisdom and compassion, reflecting not only who he was, but who I had always been. Who we had always been.

His presence was an anchor, pulling me into the present moment with the gentle force of gravity itself. My breath aligned with his. My mind emptied. My soul opened like a flower in sunlight.

I was home.

And the meditation had only just begun.

22

Inside the damp, shadow-drenched recesses of the compound, a chill clung to the air like cobwebs that never moved. Rough-hewn walls of ancient rock sweated with moisture, the earthy scent of mold and decay rising in the still air. General Horemheb sat hunched in the corner of a dim, windowless cell, the cold from the stone floor creeping into his bones as if nature itself sought to hasten his surrender.

He had been waiting.

He had known death was coming for him—an inevitable outcome sealed the moment he chose loyalty to his family over obedience to his conscience. Days earlier, he'd led a band of soldiers into foreign lands under the pretense of diplomacy, knowing all too well it was a suicide mission cloaked in the veil of duty. Ay's ultimatum had left him with no other path. He had accepted his fate.

And yet, despite the clarity of that decision, fear gnawed at him now. Not the kind of fear that charges into battle and rides with adrenaline, but the quiet kind—the cold certainty of an ending that cannot be fought.

This campaign had been unlike any Horemheb had endured. There was no battlefield here, no clash of iron or the echo of war drums. Only the crushing silence of a place buried beneath rock and time. There was no enemy in armor, but rather, an enigma in the form of a towering, godlike man.

Drunvalo.

Who—or what—was he really? The questions burned in Horemheb's mind. Was he truly a survivor of the Atlantean race Anubis once whispered about in hushed reverence? Did beings like him really seed the foundations of Egypt and other ancient civilizations, as the myths claimed? The general's heart pounded not from fear alone, but from the weight of not knowing.

Then, light.

A beam of blinding brilliance flooded the chamber, slicing through darkness like a blade. Horemheb shielded his eyes, blinking rapidly to adjust, and from the radiant veil emerged a figure—tall, commanding, and otherworldly.

Drunvalo.

Clad in shimmering black armor that gleamed with impossible precision, his very presence seemed to bend the air around him. The plating bore symbols unfamiliar to Horemheb—etched runes that shimmered like liquid mercury under the light. Not forged by earthly hands, every inch of the armor was seamless, protective, divine.

The helmet receded with a faint hiss, revealing a face as unreadable as stone. Deep-set, onyx eyes stared down at the general, devoid of emotion, as though crafted to observe but never feel.

"Why, General?" Drunvalo's voice was rich and layered, vibrating with quiet fury. "Why return with soldiers? Was my demonstration not sufficient? Do you think I wish to kill you? I do not. But you force my hand."

Horemheb, though weary and starved, straightened his back. "I had no choice. My family...." He swallowed, voice cracking with a dryness born of three days without water. "Their lives were threatened. I had to obey Ay. I meant no disrespect."

Drunvalo studied him, his expression unchanged. Yet something shifted in the air—a twitch in his jaw, a flicker behind those inscrutable eyes.

"Your leaders," he murmured, voice like steel wrapped in silk, "would sacrifice you for greed. They crave gold. Temples. Empty monuments to false gods. Fools. I am the god they worship and yet refuse to see."

The words hung heavy. Horemheb felt them in his chest, in the pit of his stomach. It was true—he could feel it. Something deep in his being resonated with the man's claim.

"Is it true then?" Horemheb asked, trembling with wonder. "Are you one of them? From Atlantis? Did your people truly build our world?"

Drunvalo tilted his head. "My people guided yours from the darkness. We gave you fire, language, order. We raised your first temples, trained your first priests. Anubis—yes, the Anubis you know—is one of us. A steward. He walked with my father before the oceans consumed our home."

The general's heart thundered. The pieces were falling into place—every myth, every story dismissed by the scribes as allegory. His mouth hung open, unsure of what to say.

"And the Order?" he finally asked. "The initiatory practices ...? They are yours?"

"Ours," Drunvalo said, stepping closer, his presence consuming the room. "Designed to unlock the infinite within the finite. Your temples are keys, your rites—maps. But you have forgotten. You've turned inward journeys into pageantry."

Horemheb felt the sting of shame.

Drunvalo continued, more passionately now. "Our temples, constructed with ratios tied to universal laws, are instruments of ascension. The one your pharaohs try to mimic—your Great Pyramid—was not built by them. It was built by us. Not for death. For awakening."

The silence that followed was not empty. It was electric.

"I didn't know," Horemheb said, voice barely above a whisper. "We were never taught."

"You were distracted by power," Drunvalo replied coldly. "Comfort. You looked outward. Always outward. Never within. That is the disease of mankind."

The general dared one final question. "Where are your people now? Why did you abandon us?"

Drunvalo's gaze softened, just slightly. "We did not abandon you. Some of us remain hidden among you. Others returned to the stars. We are stewards—not rulers. Your suffering is the crucible of your growth. We guide. We do not govern."

He turned, preparing to leave, his silhouette glowing in the doorway. But Horemheb called out.

"What will happen to me?"

Drunvalo paused. "You will live. You will return. And if you remember what I have taught you, perhaps you will inspire others to rediscover what was lost."

Horemheb, breath catching, asked one final question. "What will you do in Egypt?"

Drunvalo's voice was thunder. "I will restore balance. I will remove the head of the serpent."

And then, he vanished—leaving only the light in his wake, and the distant sound of thunder echoing through the stone halls.

23

When Anubis, Ankehesenpaaten, and I arrived at the base of the Great Pyramid, the monumental structure loomed before us like a mountain carved by gods. The setting sun's golden rays bathed the limestone blocks in firelight, casting long shadows across the sands. My heart pounded in my chest, each beat echoing like a drum of fate. I knew I had spent lifetimes preparing for this moment.

We ascended the sloping passages in silence, each step drawing me closer to the King's Chamber and the mysterious culmination of my final initiatory rite. As we entered from the Grand Gallery, a warm pulse of energy greeted me, as if the temple itself had been expecting us. The air was dense with incense, and the flicker of glowing white stones cast ethereal reflections across the polished red granite walls.

The sarcophagus stood like a sacred altar in the chamber's center, its red granite lid removed and propped against the far wall. A host of priests moved about the chamber in reverent silence, carefully withdrawing luminous stones from a large wooden crate. These mysterious stones shimmered with a soft, inner glow—pulsing like living hearts—as they were affixed to golden brackets embedded in the stone. With each stone placed, the chamber became brighter, until the space radiated with a celestial light, untouched by flame or sun.

In the back corner, a second crate held the ornate golden mask. As my eyes fell upon it, an electric shiver surged through me. The butterflies in my stomach fluttered madly. I remembered everything—the pressure of the mask, the surge of light, the visions that tore the veil between worlds. This was no ordinary exercise; I could feel it humming in my bones.

Anubis motioned gently, his eyes calm and unwavering. I stepped forward, reverence guiding my every movement. The sarcophagus yawned before me like a portal to another realm. As I prepared to enter, I instinctively turned to Anubis, awaiting his words. His voice, as always, was warm and grounded, yet it carried the weight of ancient stars.

"Tutankhamen," he said softly, his gaze locking with mine, "this exercise is unlike any that came before it. You now stand at the threshold of the creative void. Here, within this sacred chamber, your thoughts are amplified a thousandfold. Every desire you entertain will be echoed into reality."

My breath caught. I had not anticipated this. Was I truly being given the power to create? Could my thoughts possibly ripple through time and space, shaping what was to come? I looked into Anubis's eyes, searching for clarity.

"Am I to understand," I asked carefully, "that the purpose of this rite is to grant me the power to manifest my desires?"

Anubis nodded solemnly. "Yes. But you must choose wisely. You are no longer bound by the illusion of separation. You have tasted your eternal nature and glimpsed the interconnectedness of all life. In that knowledge, you must understand that nothing born of the material world can satisfy your true longing.

"Focus instead on the eternal. Manifest qualities that elevate, that harmonize, that heal. Love. Joy. Forgiveness. Gratitude. Compassion. These are the divine seeds of creation. Let these be your offering."

His words struck a chord deep within me. I had crossed the boundaries of reason and returned to a past life. The impossible had become my truth. And now I stood on the edge of something even greater. I felt the weight of this responsibility like a stone in my chest, grounding me.

"Are you saying I should focus on qualities that improve the universal experience?" I asked, my voice laced with wonder and humility.

Anubis smiled, his expression tinged with pride. "Yes, my child. You now understand. Your journey has led you here so that your soul may ripple light into eternity. Every choice you make here will affect the future's unfolding."

He paused, eyes narrowing with thoughtful gravity. "Begin by remembering the moments when you most embodied those eternal qualities. Recall the sensation of loving without condition, forgiving with an open heart, finding joy in simple truth. Let these memories become your language. From them, shape your desires."

He stepped aside, and two priests came forward with the golden mask. The mask glistened with enameled color and embedded gems, humming with latent energy. As it descended over my head, I felt the tiny stones inside press gently into my skin, radiating a pulsing warmth that spread through my body.

I lay back inside the sarcophagus as four priests heaved the granite lid into place. A dull, thunderous thud signaled my entombment. Complete darkness enveloped me. Then, the chanting began—low, harmonic tones vibrating through the stone, resonating with my breath, my heartbeat, my very being.

The air grew hot and metallic, thick with the scent of copper and leather. The gems within the mask began to glow, and I felt myself slipping into another state of consciousness. My body vanished. Only thought remained. Thought, and light.

I remembered Anubis's counsel. I turned my mind to compassion, and my chest filled with warmth. I thought of joy, and light poured from me like sunlight on water. I envisioned forgiveness, and a garden bloomed in the darkness. I conjured peace, and I heard the hush of the stars. These were not images—they were realities. I was *becoming* them.

I thought about the world I had come from—its pain, its longing, its hunger for meaning. I saw how I had been shaped by those struggles, and how I could offer something back. Not with words. Not with doctrine. But through my essence.

It became clear: I could not explain this experience. I could only embody it.

And that—that was the paradox.

I would have to become the message.

And let the universe feel it through me.

Moments later, I felt my soul being swept away as if by a great unseen wind. The mask's radiant gems pulsed, each one a portal to a place beyond time. I was no longer in the chamber. I was racing through eternity.

Faces emerged from the darkness like fireflies in a storm—millions of them, flickering in and out of view. Their eyes carried the same hollow longing I once knew. I saw a world buckling beneath the weight of misunderstanding, a collective illusion that joy could be earned through struggle, that love must be chased, and that we are alone in our pain. The future was not foreign; it was familiar. These people were me—every version of me that had ever questioned their worth or wandered in spiritual darkness.

An aching truth settled into my heart: No matter the era or advancement, humanity's central battle remained unchanged. We believed ourselves powerless in the face of adversity, blind to the divine fire housed within each soul. We mistook our separation for solitude and failed to see the golden threads that wove us together.

I understood now that I had not been invisible—I had been closed. Closed to love, closed to joy, closed to connection. But the source of light had always been within me, waiting to be uncovered.

Suddenly, the vision shifted. I stood in a modern metropolis, surrounded by glass towers and the thrumming heartbeat of industry. People rushed through the streets, faces tight with longing. A factory worker dreamed of being an executive, the executive dreamed of vanishing into simplicity. Retail workers, gas station attendants, businesspeople—each of them chasing different forms of the same elusive prize: happiness. They didn't see that joy had never been out there. It had always been within.

Then, just as swiftly, I was pulled back into the ancient past. I found myself standing in a barren expanse of Earth, untouched and primal. The air was crisp, unmarred by the scent of civilization. I was among a small tribe of builders, carving massive granite stones with primitive tools. We had no machinery, yet these stones floated into position as if weightless, guided by thought and intent alone.

Among the workers were two souls I knew well: Sara, my eternal partner, and Anubis, my guide. I seemed to lead them, or perhaps I was the student. The distinction blurred. We were building something sacred—not just shelter, but sanctuary. A birthplace of civilization. It was a marvel of harmony between effort and intuition.

Another shift. Now I was in a medieval city, perhaps London, cloaked in gray fog and the scent of coal smoke. Inside a candlelit laboratory, I watched myself—robed in deep indigo—decanting glowing liquids between delicate flasks. I was an alchemist, studying the secrets of transformation. Anubis stood at my side once more, a patient master.

"Every substance," he taught, "shares the same creative origin. By raising its vibration, you elevate its form."

We were transforming base lead into gold—but it wasn't only metal that was being transmuted. It was my soul. The lesson echoed: True change comes from within.

Lifetime after lifetime flashed before me. In each incarnation, I was a seeker—a builder of temples, a healer of hearts, an alchemist of spirit. The path varied, but the theme remained: growth, evolution, expansion. I was not here to perfect a role. I was here to perfect myself.

Anubis's voice came again, a memory vibrating through my very bones:

"The universe is always expanding. You are here to grow alongside it. Who you become is more important than any title you wear. Expansion of the soul—that is your eternal legacy."

Then I saw the answer to my most urgent question—how to heal the suffering of the world. The answer was not in invention or revolution. It was in presence. In love. In choosing, moment by moment, to embody the eternal qualities: compassion, joy, gratitude, forgiveness. Not just to understand them, but to *live* them.

The mask on my face glowed white-hot. I was no longer seeing visions—I was living revelations. I realized that by releasing my pain, I became more open. Through that openness, I could channel the eternal. That was the paradox: To change the world, I had to change nothing outside myself. I had to *become*.

And then it was over. The sarcophagus opened. Cool air kissed my skin as I rose like a phoenix from stone. I had returned.

Ankhesenpaaten rushed to me. Her embrace was trembling, her tears fresh.

"You were gone too long," she whispered. "In my dreams, Sekhmet came for you. I feared I had lost you forever."

I held her tightly, gently pressing my forehead to hers. "You could never lose me. What we share is eternal. Even if time parts us, we are never truly separated."

Her trembling softened. She nodded, finding peace in my promise. Then her eyes searched mine.

"Tell me," she asked, "what did you choose to manifest? What future awaits us?"

Her question struck me. She had been waiting not just for my return, but for an answer—a glimpse into the soul I had rediscovered.

Anubis, standing just beyond the shadows, leaned in with subtle anticipation.

I turned to her and said, "I chose to open my heart. I chose to become a living expression of the qualities that are eternal."

Anubis smiled with unmistakable pride. "A noble choice, Tutankhamen. Perhaps the noblest. I could not have chosen better myself."

Then, with a soft bow, he added, "When you're ready, I must speak with you privately. There's an urgent matter we must discuss."

Though the request carried weight, his eyes offered no alarm—only clarity.

"Of course," I said, meeting his gaze. "How could I refuse the one who helped me find myself again?"

24

Later that evening, as the veil of dusk settled gently over the palace grounds, Anubis returned in silence. The tension in his shoulders was unmistakable. We met on the upper balcony—our private retreat high above the bustle of court life—where the cool, dry night air stirred gently around us.

The view before us was breathtaking. The full moon hung low and luminous over the desert horizon, casting a silvery sheen across the still waters of the Nile, which shimmered like a ribbon of obsidian. Stars, like celestial guardians, pierced the inky sky above, while the smooth white limestone of the Great Pyramid reflected the moonlight in a golden haze. It glowed like an ancient lantern against the vast darkness of the valley, a silent sentinel bearing witness to the mysteries of time.

A warm breeze rose from the desert floor, laced with the scent of sand, date palms, and distant fire. It carried an unusual electric tingle—subtle but unnerving. I turned toward Anubis. He was not himself. Gone was the serene and steady man I had always known. In his place sat a restless figure, his eyes flickering with unease, scanning the shadows with hurried glances. His crimson ceremonial robe fluttered against the wind, and the tension in his jaw betrayed the storm brewing behind his calm facade.

"Tutankhamen," he said, his voice soft but firm, as if carefully balancing urgency and restraint. "Please, listen closely. What I am about to tell you is not only of great importance—it is destiny."

He leaned in, lowering his voice to a whisper that barely rose above the wind. "Our time together is drawing to a close."

My heart tightened. Something had shifted—within him, within the air, within fate itself. I stared into his eyes and saw panic flickering like torchlight. The sight of fear in Anubis, my unshakeable guide, unnerved me.

"What do you mean?" I asked, the words catching in my throat. "What is happening?"

Anubis looked over his shoulder, scanning the shadows. Then he turned back to me, the weight of a thousand secrets in his gaze.

"I have known from the beginning," he said, "that you are not the same Tutankhamen who entered the sarcophagus three weeks ago. You carry memories, experiences, and awareness from a different time. I recognized it the moment you opened your eyes in the pit."

I remained silent, my pulse thudding in my ears.

"You are one of the chosen," he continued. "Chosen to return to the past at the end of a great cycle, to help fulfill an ancient prophecy. The prophecy of the Great Shift."

"The Great Shift?" I echoed.

"Yes," Anubis said solemnly. "A transformation of consciousness that will affect all of mankind. It will be a time of upheaval, of fear, of great disconnection. Humanity will forget its divine nature. It will need the guidance of those like you—initiates who have walked many lifetimes and unlocked the truth of who they are."

His words hit me with a quiet thunder. I could hardly breathe. Me? Chosen for such a monumental task?

I shook my head, suddenly overwhelmed with self-doubt. "But how do you know it's me? Why me?"

Anubis leaned forward, his voice steady despite the fear in his eyes. "Because I have known you across lifetimes. Our bond is eternal. I have guided you before, and I will again. Each time, you grow stronger. Each time, you remember more."

I stared into the desert night, trying to make sense of everything. The pyramid pulsed in the distance like a beating heart.

"How many more of these experiences will I have?" I asked.

"That," he said with a solemn nod, "is up to you. The more you awaken to your true identity, the more you will remember. And with memory comes power."

"Power?" I asked, glancing back at him. "Are you speaking of my mental abilities?"

He smiled gently, the warmth of his old self returning briefly. "Not just mental. Spiritual, emotional, intuitive. The ability to shape reality from within. You have already begun. But the rest is waiting."

I nodded slowly. "How much time do I have left here?"

He looked to the horizon, where distant thunderclouds now roamed over the desert like dark ships. "Not long. Perhaps moments. Before you go, I must ask something of you."

"Anything," I replied without hesitation.

"In a future lifetime," he said, placing a hand on mine, "I may need your help. I may be lost, buried beneath layers of illusion and forgetfulness. Promise me that when the time comes, you will help me remember."

Emotion surged within me. "Of course. I will find you. How will I know where to look?"

"You will know," he said with certainty. "Follow your heart. It will lead you to me, as it always has."

We sat in silence for a moment longer, two old souls staring into the swirling unknown. Then, as if swept away by the very winds of time, everything faded. Anubis's face softened into sorrow and hope, and then dissolved into blackness.

I was gone.

25

The stars hung like a tapestry of silver fire across the Egyptian night sky, their light casting glints off the still waters of the Nile. On the palace balcony, under the cool breath of a midnight breeze, Anubis stood in silent contemplation, the tension in the air thickening with every passing second. His gaze swept the valley below, sensing an imminent storm far greater than weather. Then, without a whisper of warning, Drunvalo appeared behind Tutankhamen, as if stepping through a veil of shadow.

Clad in glistening black armor etched with celestial runes and symbols of a forgotten power, Drunvalo moved with terrifying speed. The moonlight gleamed across his horned helm and polished pauldrons, transforming him into a god of war descended from the stars. In the blink of an eye, his armored hand clamped around the young pharaoh's skull, lifting him into the air as though he weighed nothing. Lightning crackled from Drunvalo's gauntlets, surging into Tutankhamen's body in violent pulses. The boy convulsed, his screams swallowed by the crackling energy before he fell silent, lifeless, and limp.

Anubis froze in horror. His chest tightened, not with fear for himself, but for what had just been unleashed. Drunvalo let Tutankhamen's body fall to the stone floor like a discarded garment. His eyes, glowing faintly with cruel light, locked on Anubis. The enforcer's voice came low and cold:

"Anubis, your failure to restore harmony has triggered a chain reaction that will ripple far beyond this moment."

Anubis's heart sank. The inevitability of this encounter had long been foretold in the hidden scrolls. He had always known Drunvalo might return, but the attack's brutal swiftness had shattered every expectation. Still, he stood tall.

They were brothers, of a sort—both children of Atlantis, both born of light and knowledge now twisted by time and corruption. Once, their families had trained together as initiates beneath the golden domes of the Atlantean citadel, mastering sacred sciences and the ancient rites. But while Anubis had remained loyal to the cosmic laws of balance, Drunvalo had grown cold, his heart hardened by centuries of pain and disillusionment.

"Drunvalo," Anubis said, his voice steady, though his sorrow threatened to seep through, "you've overstepped. You were never sent here to judge or destroy. You were a steward, like me, a guide to humanity—not its executioner."

Drunvalo's armored chest rose and fell with deep, controlled breaths. He had not expected resistance, especially from Anubis. His gaze narrowed.

"I tire of your ideals, old friend. The world is in chaos. You've let the Egyptians spiral into decadence. Their thirst for power mirrors the arrogance of Atlantis. If I don't intervene, history will repeat itself."

Anubis shook his head, disappointment wrinkling his brow. "So you kill a boy? A boy who was not as he seemed? Do you even realize what you've done?"

Drunvalo's stance faltered. His brow creased. "What do you mean? Who was he?"

Anubis stepped forward, the night wind tousling his robes. His voice, though quiet, carried the weight of eternity.

"He was not just Tutankhamen. He was an initiate from the future. One of the chosen, returned to fulfill the prophecy. You killed him before he could remember who he truly was."

Drunvalo's mouth tightened into a line. The tales of the Great Shift, the return of the old initiates, echoed from his childhood. His father had believed them. Told him stories by firelight of the day when time itself would bend and the greatest among them would return. Drunvalo had dismissed them as myths. But now ... doubt twisted inside him like a blade.

"You're certain?"

Anubis nodded solemnly. "I recognized him the moment he emerged from the sarcophagus. We have shared lifetimes. I have watched him rise again and again, always at the right time. You just severed one of our most important timelines."

Drunvalo turned away, pacing toward the balcony's edge. Below, the Nile rolled on as if nothing had changed. But everything had. He knew the laws of causality. The Council would not forgive this. Unless ... he erased the last witness.

He turned back, his eyes hardening into steel. "Then you understand why I cannot let you live."

Anubis didn't flinch. His eyes were calm, accepting.

"I've seen this moment in visions. I am ready. Do what you must, but know this: You and I will meet again, in another place, another time. Perhaps our roles will be reversed. Perhaps you will be the one begging for understanding."

Drunvalo hesitated, his gauntlet trembling at his side. But he couldn't allow hesitation. With a flash of light, he lunged forward.

The stars above flickered in silence, bearing witness to a tragedy that echoed across time.

And then, only silence remained on the balcony of the Nile.

26

I drifted back into consciousness, as if surfacing from beneath an ocean of dreams, only to find myself wrapped once more in the cold, timeless stillness of the King's Chamber. The air was thick and unmoving, dense with the weight of ages, and I immediately felt the throbbing ache pulsing through my skull. My head felt like it had been struck by stone, and I was lying flat inside the granite sarcophagus, its rigid interior pressing against my spine.

Everything was dark, except for the faint, anemic light from the chamber's lone artificial source. It cast eerie shadows across the soot-coated walls and ceiling, which loomed overhead like ancient, silent sentinels. The once-smooth limestone was blackened by time and smoke, the scars of countless rituals and centuries of dust leaving it cloaked in a funereal veil. My eyes found the jagged, triangular hole in the side of the sarcophagus—the same damaged corner I had noted when I first arrived. The familiarity of it confirmed what my gut already knew: I had returned to my life in the future.

A low-grade anxiety began to coil inside my chest. I didn't know how long I had been gone or what time it was now. My memories of the pyramid tour were hazy, disjointed, like faded photographs caught in a sandstorm. What I did know was that lying inside the sarcophagus was definitely against the rules. The thought of being caught in such a sacred, restricted place sent a fresh jolt of adrenaline through my veins.

But I didn't rush. I stayed still, holding my breath, letting the silence envelop me. Every minute that passed without footsteps or voices confirmed I was alone. I listened for the slightest echo, the faintest shuffle of shoes against stone, but the chamber held nothing but the soft drumbeat of my heart. After what felt like an eternity, I decided to move.

Carefully, I slid out of the sarcophagus, my muscles stiff and reluctant, as though they, too, were unsure if we had truly returned. The cool air clung to my skin as I crept into the Grand Gallery. The passage loomed before me like the throat of some great beast, its steep incline and rough-hewn steps forcing me to grip the cold steel handrails tightly. I moved with painstaking care, my footsteps deliberately silent.

The ancient stones, slick with dust and worn smooth by time, seemed to breathe beneath me. My senses were sharpened to a razor's edge. I scanned every dark recess, every flicker of light and shadow, fully expecting a security guard to materialize from the gloom.

But no one came.

Finally, I reached the pyramid's exit and stepped outside. The warm breath of the desert night greeted me like an old friend. Overhead, a tapestry of stars unfolded across the heavens, bright and impossibly close. The full moon hovered like a silent guardian, casting silver light over the sands and illuminating the ancient monuments in ghostly brilliance. The Great Pyramid rose behind me like a mountain of shadow, eternal and unmoved.

The site was completely abandoned. Not a soul in sight.

I began moving, quickly and silently, across the compound. The gritty sand crunched beneath my shoes as I put distance between myself and the looming pyramid. My eyes darted left and right, heart pounding in anticipation of a voice shouting from the dark.

Nothing.

Once I reached the outer perimeter, I found myself in total darkness. The city lights glowed faintly on the horizon like a mirage, beckoning me home. I kept walking, guided only by moonlight and the occasional shimmer from the distant skyline. I felt like I had stepped into another dimension—a sacred borderland between worlds.

I followed the highway I had come in on. The road was silent, a ribbon of black stretching endlessly ahead, bordered by vast emptiness. I saw no headlights, heard no sounds of tires on asphalt, not even the chirp of desert creatures. All that seemed to exist was me, the whisper of wind, and the throb in my temples.

When I looked skyward again, I felt awe stir in my chest. The stars seemed impossibly vivid, a celestial map painted across the heavens. I recalled the ancient belief that the Nile and its sacred architecture mirrored the constellation of Orion's belt. The alignment felt intentional, powerful. I whispered to myself: "As above, so below."

The walk stretched on. My energy waned. My limbs felt heavier with each step. I muttered, half-joking, half-desperate, "I sure wish someone would come along and give me a ride to my hotel."

Walking felt futile. The road was barren, lifeless. But just as I crested a small rise, two brilliant beams of bluish-purple light appeared on the horizon, cutting through the dark like twin swords. A sound followed: the screaming growl of a high-revving engine.

The vehicle was flying down the road, closing the distance between us in seconds. I jumped to the side, just as a white BMW coupe tore past, its roar deafening. The blast of air from its wake hit me like a tidal wave, nearly knocking me over. My heart pounded in my chest. That had been too close.

I watched the car disappear into the distance, the taillights shrinking to pinpricks. Despite the scare, a glimmer of hope returned. I figured the road had a dead-end, so the driver would have to double back. I stayed close to the shoulder, eyes straining in the dark.

Ten minutes later, the howl of the engine returned. This time, the lights slowed. The BMW coasted toward me and came to a stop, the passenger window already rolled down. A man with dark hair, a mischievous smile, and a hint of boyish charm leaned over from the driver's seat.

"Sorry I missed you the first time," he said, chuckling. "Was going a bit too fast. You all right? Need a ride?"

I couldn't help but laugh at the absurdity of it all. The man seemed harmless, and I was too tired to be cautious. He reminded me of my younger self—reckless, curious, alive.

"Yeah, I'd be eternally grateful. I'm beat, and Cairo is still a long way off."

The man reached across and popped the door open. "Ahmed," he said, shaking my hand.

"John," I replied, stepping into the car's cool interior.

"You look like you've been wrestling with the desert gods themselves," he joked.

"Something like that," I said with a smile.

As soon as the door clicked shut, Ahmed punched the accelerator. The engine roared to life again, and we surged forward. I leaned back, letting the wind from the open windows rush over my face. The thrill of speed, the comfort of a seat, the laughter of a stranger beside me—all of it felt like a strange dream at the edge of awakening.

I watched the stars blur overhead and let the moment wash over me, grateful for the ride, for the strange and sacred journey, and for the road still ahead.

27

The sun was already dipping low in the sky when I finally stirred from the thick cocoon of sleep. My eyes cracked open to the warm amber light slanting through the hotel's heavy curtains. I groaned softly, a dull throb still pulsing at the back of my skull from the previous night's ordeal. Time had melted away since I'd returned from the Great Pyramid, and judging by the soft shadows painted on the walls, it was already late afternoon.

I hadn't planned anything for the day—how could I, after what I'd just endured? My heart still struggled to piece together the fragments of what felt like another life. Had I truly lived through a past incarnation, or had I fallen prey to a vivid hallucination in the pitch-black belly of the pyramid? I couldn't say. But the sensation that something fundamental within me had changed was undeniable. My body felt foreign, humming with some ancient, dormant energy now reawakened. Even the people I passed in the hotel lobby earlier had eyed me with puzzled interest, as if I radiated a frequency they couldn't quite place.

I needed time to think, to reflect—and more than anything, I needed to eat. After hours spent drifting between timelines and lifetimes, I craved the simple comfort of a good meal. The hotel boasted a highly rated, upscale restaurant, and despite my modest wardrobe, I decided to treat myself to a rare evening of indulgence. Slipping into my cleanest outfit—khakis and a light-blue golf shirt—I took a deep breath and made my way down to the restaurant.

The lobby was already beginning to buzz with life as the dinner hour approached. When I arrived at the entrance of the sleek, modern dining space, I was surprised to find a line of guests spilling through the foyer and out onto the steps. The crowd looked polished and elite, draped in designer dresses and tailored suits. I hesitated. Maybe I should just order room service. But something held me in place—a quiet pull, as if fate had laid a thread before me, urging me to follow.

As I stepped across the threshold into the waiting area, an odd sensation prickled across my skin. The chatter of conversation dimmed. Heads turned. One by one, people stopped mid-sentence, utensils suspended midair, wine glasses paused inches from lips. The room fell eerily quiet. I slowed my pace, suddenly self-conscious under the weight of so many stares.

Had someone important walked in behind me? I glanced over my shoulder, half-expecting to see a diplomat or a movie star entering after me. But the doorway remained empty. The moment stretched unnaturally long before I realized: It was me. I was the focus of their attention.

I tried to shrug it off, unsure how to process the wave of silent scrutiny pressing against me. As I approached the hostess stand, even she seemed caught off guard. Her poised smile faltered as she took me in, eyes wide and uncertain.

"Good evening," I said gently, trying to break the spell. "Looks like you're pretty packed. How long is the wait for one?"

She blinked, then shook herself slightly, glancing down at the seating chart like she had forgotten how to read it. "Um … are you dining alone?" she asked, her voice soft and almost reverent. "Can I get a name?"

"John Fullman," I replied.

Still dazed, she searched the list, then looked back up at me. "We have a seat at the bar open right now, if that would be okay?"

I nodded. "The bar is fine. Thank you."

She grabbed a menu, gestured for me to follow, and led me through the restaurant. As I passed the diners, I felt their gazes trail me like spotlights. Conversations had halted entirely. The air was thick with curiosity, awe—maybe even reverence. I had once been a boy-king, clothed in gold and worshiped by millions, but nothing had prepared me for this.

The restaurant was sleek and modern, all steel beams and shimmering glass sculptures, like a shrine to contemporary luxury. But I felt like an artifact out of time. My simple clothes stood in stark contrast to the polished clientele, yet none of them seemed to care. In fact, their eyes followed me with the same intensity one might give royalty.

The hostess placed a menu in front of me and began to walk away, only to hesitate. She turned back slowly, eyes flickering with something unsaid.

"Mr. Fullman," she said at last, her voice uncertain. "I feel silly asking this, but … are you someone famous?"

I was caught off guard. I had expected a comment about my attire, not this.

"Not at all," I replied, amused. "Why do you ask?"

She looked embarrassed, almost frustrated. "It's just ... everyone is staring at you. I've never seen anyone command a room like that. Celebrities come through here all the time, but you ... it's different."

"What exactly do you mean?" I pressed, intrigued.

She gestured subtly to the still-silent room behind me. "Look around. Haven't you noticed? They haven't taken their eyes off you since you walked in."

Trying not to make her feel foolish, I nodded. "I did notice, but I thought maybe it was because I'm dressed for the golf course."

She laughed, the tension easing from her posture. "Well, yes, you are underdressed. But that's not it. There's something ... about you. Something I can't explain."

Her words settled in my chest like a whisper from the past. Whatever had happened in the King's Chamber—whatever I had remembered or become—wasn't just lingering inside me. It was radiating outward, reshaping the world's perception of me in ways I hadn't yet begun to understand.

28

It wasn't until the next day at the airport—amid the chaos of rolling luggage, overhead announcements, and the scent of jet fuel lingering in the air—that I began to grasp the truth of what had happened to me. Something deep within had changed. The transformation I had undergone during my journey through time wasn't fading. In fact, it was growing more apparent with each passing moment. Whatever I had become in that other lifetime had not been left behind in the past. It had traveled back with me. And everyone seemed to notice.

Gone were the days of invisibility, of blending anonymously into crowds. Now, strangers gravitated toward me like moths to a flame. They couldn't take their eyes off me, and conversations dissolved into silence when I entered a room, like the air had shifted and everyone could sense something beyond their understanding. The energy I carried was magnetic, inexplicable, yet undeniable.

And somehow, it felt right. As strange as the attention was, it wasn't invasive. It was reverent. People felt something in my presence—a quiet warmth, an ancient love, a healing comfort. These weren't traits I had tried to cultivate. They simply flowed out from the center of me, as if I had become a conduit for something greater, something divine. I couldn't help but wonder: Had this all stemmed from my final exercise within the Great Pyramid? Was it the harmony and balance I had achieved there that now radiated outward, shifting others without a word?

Despite the mystery surrounding my new condition, I felt no fear. Only a quiet awe. Perhaps, like Anubis, my presence now stirred remembrance in others—a faint echo of something eternal.

The bustling terminal of Cairo International Airport buzzed around me, but my mind was focused elsewhere. I had promised Anubis I would help him, and I intended to keep that promise. Yet I had no idea where to begin. There were no maps to guide me, no addresses scribbled on scraps of parchment. I had to trust something larger than logic would direct me—a kind of guidance I was still learning to follow.

Lost in thought, I almost missed the man and woman trying to get my attention. They stood off to the side, their posture hesitant, their eyes wide with a mix of recognition and disbelief. It wasn't until the man gently touched my arm that I realized they were speaking to me.

"Excuse me," he said, his voice laced with tentative familiarity, "but weren't you part of the late afternoon tour at the Great Pyramid a few days ago?"

As soon as he spoke, I recognized them—an American couple I'd taken a photo of in front of the pyramid's monumental entrance. I smiled, slightly sheepish.

"Yes," I replied. "I was on the four-thirty tour. Good to see you again."

The man let out a short breath, relieved. "I knew it. You disappeared from the group that day. They were looking for you everywhere. My wife and I were worried. Glad to see you're okay. It's never a good thing when American tourists vanish overseas."

We exchanged a few more words; then they hurried off to their gate. I settled into a nearby chair, my thoughts spinning. And then, a flicker of movement drew my eye to a row of televisions mounted along the wall. The bold crimson lettering of a breaking news alert seized my attention.

On CNN, a reporter with polished poise and concerned blue eyes addressed the camera. "Breaking news today: The global tech market has taken a nosedive following the indefinite delay of the historic merger between Global Media Network and Orion Data Systems. The delay stems from the sudden disappearance of GMN's founder and CEO, William Allbright."

The screen shifted to an image of Allbright—and I froze.

There, in perfect clarity, was the man I knew as Anubis.

The report continued. Allbright had vanished shortly after his wife and son were presumed dead, their private company jet lost somewhere over the Atlantic. His CFO, Earl Buckingham, stood at a podium, delivering the grim announcement with all the gravitas of a seasoned statesman.

"When the search was officially called off," he said, "William disappeared. We haven't heard from him since. For now, all negotiations and merger proceedings have been put on hold."

My breath caught in my throat. I couldn't believe what I was hearing. William Allbright—Anubis—had endured a loss uncannily similar to my own. His disappearance wasn't just an escape. It was a retreat into the shadows, a soul in mourning, trying to reconcile grief and destiny.

So, now I knew where to begin.

He was out there, hiding from a world that was searching for him. But I wasn't the world. I was something else. I was part of his story. And he was part of mine.

I leaned back in the airport chair, the hum of travel and time folding around me like the beginning of a dream. Somewhere in the world, Anubis waited.

And I would find him.

29

Just as I was beginning to lose myself in thought, a subtle movement at the edge of my vision tugged at my attention. There, emerging from the shifting river of travelers, was a familiar figure—the same weary man I had encountered weeks earlier at Heathrow. His shoulders were slightly hunched, his pace deliberate, like a man trudging against the weight of something unseen. And yet, somehow, he was walking directly toward me.

He lowered himself into the seat beside mine without a word, the leather cushion creaking faintly beneath him. His eyes remained fixed ahead, scanning the flow of harried passengers rushing past us. For a long moment, he said nothing, as if drawing strength from the quiet motion around us. When he finally spoke, his voice was low and flat, drained of emotion, like a violin played without a bow.

"It seems you and I are on the same journey. Although, now it's as if our roles have been reversed."

He turned to me then, and the weight of his gaze caught me off guard. His eyes, once sharp and proud, now brimmed with sorrow. That was when it hit me: He was William Allbright. The words he spoke suddenly made sense.

"In what way do you mean?" I asked, already suspecting the answer but wanting to hear it from him.

A faint smile touched his lips—not one of joy, but of weary understanding. "I saw you in London. You were invisible then, just another face among a sea of travelers. But now ... now you shine like a beacon. Everyone sees you. Everyone *feels* you."

Sadness was in his voice, a quiet longing. He had noticed the change in me, perhaps even before I had fully acknowledged it myself. And he was right: Something in me had shifted. Energy flowed through me differently now. I felt open in ways I never had before.

I met his eyes and decided not to play coy. "I saw a news story about you, just minutes ago. You do know that a lot of people are looking for you, don't you?"

He blinked, startled by my directness, then followed my glance to the nearby television tuned to CNN. His expression darkened.

"Damn. So I've made the news again," he muttered bitterly. "I guess that's what happens when your company triggers a global panic."

He shook his head, and the anger slowly drained from him. When he spoke again, his tone had shifted to one of aching vulnerability.

"But honestly, I don't care about any of that. Not anymore. The board, the shareholders, the press ... they only care about one thing—money. And I can't stomach any of it right now."

His shoulders sagged under invisible burdens. He seemed smaller somehow, like a man slowly collapsing under the weight of his own legend. I saw in him not the mogul the world knew, but a man stripped of pretense, searching for something real.

"If you don't mind my asking," I said gently, "what *are* you interested in now, Mr. Allbright?"

He turned toward me, eyes narrowing as if trying to read my intentions. A long pause passed before he answered.

"Call me William. Please."

I extended my hand. "John. John Fullman."

We shook. His grip was firm but cold, like a man still unsure of his footing. But something in that gesture seemed to ground him. He sat up straighter, his voice steadier.

"To be honest, John, I don't really know what I'm interested in anymore."

Then, just as quickly, his energy receded. His shoulders slumped again, his gaze drifting toward the polished floor.

I leaned in, hoping to reach him. "So, why Egypt? Of all places to disappear to, why here?"

His eyes flicked toward me, wary, measuring. Clearly, the question had struck a chord.

"That's a complicated question," he said slowly, his voice barely above a whisper. "But let me ask you this: Have you ever felt pulled somewhere, like something—*someone*—was drawing you in a direction you never would have chosen for yourself?"

I nodded. "Absolutely."

He studied my face for any sign of mockery, then pressed on.

"No, I mean *really* pulled. Dragged, even. Like the Universe had made up its mind, and your opinion didn't matter."

"That's exactly how I ended up here," I admitted. "Still on that path, in fact."

Relief flickered across his features. A deep breath filled his chest. Then came the first true smile I had seen from him.

"Well, John, that makes two of us. I don't fully understand why, but I *had* to come here. Something inside me just *knew*. And when I stepped off the plane … it was like I had come home. These temples, these stones, these deserts—they feel like pieces of my own story, somehow. Does that sound insane to you?"

I looked into his eyes, seeing the reflection of a path I myself had walked.

"No," I said. "In fact, what you're saying is more true than you realize."

He studied me intently, sensing I was holding something back.

"You know something. You're not telling me everything."

"We're walking similar paths," I said. "And we're not walking them alone."

He fell silent, staring at me with wide eyes. Then he laughed softly, but it quickly gave way to frustration.

"None of this makes sense, John. I sound like I've lost my mind."

"You haven't," I said firmly. "You're waking up to something. Something ancient. Something powerful."

William looked away, struggling to reconcile the rising tide of emotion within him. "It's just … hard. I feel like I'm drowning in questions and have no one to talk to. No one who would understand."

"You're not alone in this," I said, placing a hand gently on his shoulder. "You just need to trust what's rising inside you. Let go. Listen to your heart. That's how I made it through."

Before he could respond, the airport intercom crackled to life.

"Ladies and gentlemen, we will now begin the boarding process for American Airlines flight 1732 to Heathrow International Airport in London...."

William wiped the corners of his eyes with his sleeve, then turned back to me, eyes glassy but grateful.

"Where are you seated, John?"

"Coach. 22B."

He frowned, shaking his head. "No way. Let me see what I can do. I have more airline points than I know what to do with. We're finishing this conversation at 30,000 feet."

For the first time, I felt like the two of us weren't just passengers on the same flight, but pilgrims on the same sacred journey—a journey neither of us had chosen, but both of us had been called to complete.

30

As fate would have it, William Allbright and I did, indeed, find ourselves seated side-by-side in the plush comfort of first class on our overnight flight to London's Heathrow International Airport. The moment I sank into the deep leather seat beside him, I could feel the calm anticipation of the journey ahead. The muted lighting of the cabin, paired with the subtle hum of the engines and the gentle clink of fine glassware, provided the perfect backdrop for a conversation unlike any other.

Almost immediately, we fell into a rhythm. The conversation flowed with surprising ease, beginning with harmless small talk but soon diving into deeper waters. We talked at length, peeling back the layers of our lives like old friends reconnecting after lifetimes apart. I shared parts of my story with him—selective pieces of my experience that hinted at the mysteries I had uncovered without revealing the full scope of my transformation. Still, what I did share seemed to resonate with him on a profound level.

Time slipped by unnoticed. We spoke as the stars outside our window gave way to the soft glow of dawn, the golden light cresting over the curve of the earth and seeping through the tiny windows. Only then, as we reached up to pull the blinds closed, did we realize sleep had eluded us entirely. Yet neither of us seemed to mind.

A warmth existed between us—an unspoken understanding that we were each playing a role in something far larger than ourselves.

After landing, we parted briefly to manage customs and collect our bearings. I had a five-hour layover before my connecting flight, and to my surprise—and perhaps his own—William chose to stay behind at the airport rather than continue on immediately. He found a quiet little coffee shop tucked inside the bustling terminal, and we met there shortly after.

Nestled into a secluded corner booth beneath hanging lamps and surrounded by the low murmur of travelers and the hiss of espresso machines, we resumed our conversation. I began to explain the arc of my research and how it had led me through ancient texts, sacred geometry, and the silent whispers of the world's oldest temples. As I spoke, William leaned forward with the quiet intensity of someone who had been waiting all his life to hear these things articulated.

To my surprise, he shared that he, too, had long held a fascination with the esoteric traditions of the mystery schools. He told me of his travels—to Machu Picchu, Delphi, and Angkor Wat—seeking answers he couldn't quite articulate. His eyes shone with recognition as I described the unbroken thread connecting ancient temples across cultures and continents.

Though I sensed he wasn't yet ready to grasp the true depth of our relationship or the reality of who he really was, I could see the gears turning behind his eyes. He was remembering something—perhaps not consciously, but deep within, something dormant was stirring.

Every new revelation sparked an ember within him. His shoulders straightened, the tension in his brow softened, and he began to ask questions—real questions, as if awakening from a long and restless sleep. Clearly, this knowledge was not foreign, but familiar to him. Like an old language slowly returning to the tongue.

I knew I would have to tread carefully. A time would come when I would reveal the deeper truths to him—about his past lives, his forgotten power, his role in the unfolding of a much grander design. But for now, I simply planted seeds. I spoke of the mind's untapped potential, of the hidden science taught within the mystery schools, and of the possibility of awakening the soul's ancient memory.

Before long, the overhead announcements reminded me it was time to prepare for my next flight. William and I exchanged contact information, and I promised to stay in touch—to be a guide when he was ready for more. I made him a solemn vow: to help him navigate the storm of his present circumstances and uncover the eternal truth buried within him.

As I rose to leave, I looked back one last time. William stood at the coffee shop's exit, tall and composed, his eyes no longer heavy with grief but alive with purpose. He stepped into the morning light and walked to the sleek black limousine waiting for him outside. The driver opened the door, and William paused for a moment before getting in. He turned his head, offered me a silent nod of gratitude, and then disappeared behind the tinted glass as the car pulled away.

I watched until the limousine vanished into the stream of traffic, knowing our paths would cross again. What had started as a chance encounter had become the beginning of a shared journey—one that neither of us could have predicted, yet both of us were destined to walk.

EPILOGUE

Nearly two years had slipped through the hourglass since I had sat across from William Allbright in that quiet, sun-drenched coffee shop tucked inside Heathrow Airport. And yet, it felt as if no time had passed at all. The tide of miracles rolling through my life had not crested—in fact, they seemed to swell with increasing frequency and intensity. From the moment I said goodbye to William, a new chapter had begun, for both of us. A strange and invisible thread connected our paths, guiding us through a series of experiences more surreal than anything either of us could have imagined.

Now, here we were—reunited once more. Not in a crowded airport terminal, but standing amid the ancient, time-worn stones of Stonehenge. The wind whipped around us, rustling the tall grass in soft waves, and the sky above was a heavy canvas of shifting silver clouds. We stood in the shadow of monoliths that had witnessed the birth and collapse of civilizations, their presence humming with an ancient, unseen energy.

I couldn't ignore the strange sense of familiarity pulsing through me. Just as the King's Chamber in the Great Pyramid had beckoned me like a forgotten dream, Stonehenge now called to something deep within me—something primal, timeless. And oddly enough, William was experiencing a mirror image of my own sensations. His transformation over the last two years had been nothing short of remarkable. Gone was the shattered man I had met by chance in an airport. He now stood tall, shoulders squared, with a steady glow behind his eyes that hinted at profound inner clarity.

William looked over the stones with reverence and wonder, his gaze lingering on each slab as though he were reacquainting himself with old friends. "I still can't believe this is my first time here," he said, his voice soft and almost disbelieving. "Born in London, traveled the world … and yet I never made it here until now. Tell me again—why do you believe this place is connected to the Great Pyramid? Something about a mathematical code?"

I smiled, not because the question amused me, but because his curiosity mirrored my own from years ago. "Yes," I replied, my eyes scanning the central ring of stones. "There's a shared frequency—a geometric resonance. Both structures are built on the same principles of balance and harmony. Those aren't just philosophical ideas; they're keys—keys to unlocking consciousness itself."

William nodded slowly, letting the words wash over him. He turned away, his eyes drinking in the landscape. Meanwhile, I was focused on one thing: the center stone. I had seen it countless times in my dreams—a perfectly rounded, dark gray slab nestled beneath overgrowth. It was the stone that would unlock this site's true potential, just as the sarcophagus had in the King's Chamber. Somewhere beneath the tangled blanket of weeds, I knew it was waiting.

I crouched, hands brushing aside the tall, dry grasses and ivy-like weeds that had crept over centuries. My fingers met cool stone, smooth and slightly indented at the center. I paused, breath catching in my throat. It was exactly as I had seen it—almost too perfect to believe. A jolt of adrenaline surged through me, like lightning snapping through my veins.

With urgency and care, I uncovered more of the stone, my heart thudding louder with each handful of debris I cleared. "William!" I called out, voice breaking through the wind. I looked up to see him a dozen paces away, still circling the outer stones, lost in thought. "Come here! I've found it! The stone—it's real! Are you sure you're ready for this?"

He hesitated for a beat, then turned toward me, visibly startled by the shift in my tone. The look on my face must have betrayed just how serious this was. His expression flickered—uncertainty, curiosity, and something else—something deeper. Destiny, perhaps.

He made his way toward me, eyes flicking from my face to the half-revealed stone. "I'm as ready as I'll ever be," he said, though his voice wavered slightly.

He had no idea what was coming. And truth be told, neither did I—not fully. But the energy in the air had shifted. The stones around us suddenly felt closer, heavier, as if they were leaning in, listening. Somewhere between the folds of time and memory, something ancient had begun to stir again.

And this time, we would face it together.

AFTERWORD

The Path of Fire, Balance, and Light
A Personal Reflection from the Author

There is a truth I can no longer withhold: This book is not just a story I wrote. It is the story I lived. The chambers of the Great Pyramid, the dark night of the soul, the strange mirrors of past lifetimes and cosmic memories—each element rose from the landscape of my own inner transformation. I didn't simply imagine this journey.... I walked it. Crawling at times. Collapsing in tears. Rising in awe.

What you've just read was never meant to be a work of fiction. It was a map—a mythic template drawn from the raw experience of surviving my own spiritual crisis. In 2009, I entered the fire. Everything I thought I was shattered. My relationship ended, my mother died in a fire, and I lost everything financially. From that moment, my identity, my beliefs, and my life as I knew it crumbled beneath the weight of something I couldn't name but could no longer avoid. I now understand that what I entered was the first chamber of the pyramid: the chamber of **the Dark Night of the Soul**.

The First Chamber – The Death of the Old Self

The dark night doesn't announce its arrival. It doesn't come with a guidebook or a gentle knock at the door. It arrives as a storm. A loss. A breakdown. It is the moment when the old self begins to die, and everything familiar becomes foreign.

I resisted it at first. I fought against the pain. But the truth of that first chamber is that resistance only deepens the suffering. The dark night calls us to **surrender**, not because we are weak, but because our strength must be realigned with our soul. As John faced sensory deprivation and the loss of his ego-self within the pyramid, I too faced a void—an abyss of uncertainty. It was terrifying. And yet it was sacred.

The old identity needed to die. I had to let go of who I thought I was to remember who I truly am. If you are reading these words and you feel like you are in that same space of unraveling, I promise you there is light waiting beyond the collapse. Stay with the fire. Let it burn away the illusion.

The Second Chamber – The Balance Between Darkness and Light

What came next was the silence after the storm. The second chamber was where John discovered weightlessness, neutrality—a still point between opposing forces. This is the chamber where you come face to face with your polarities. Your inner conflicts. Your judgments. Your self-abandonment and your self-protection.

In my own journey, this stage was where I stopped asking, "Why is this happening to me?" and started asking, "What is this trying to teach me?"

I had to reckon with my own shadow—my fears, my pride, my wounds—and bring them into balance with the parts of me I had rejected. This is the space where you stop running from the dark and start listening to it. You stop over-identifying with the light and start integrating it with humility.

Balance is not stasis. It is a living dance. And when we learn to stand in the center, we stop swinging wildly between extremes and begin to embody truth.

The Third Chamber – The Merging with the Higher Self

And then comes the miracle. The third chamber is where you meet the eternal part of you—the Higher Self. It is the place where sacred memory returns, where soul wisdom reawakens, where the light of who you've always been floods your awareness.

I remember the moment this awakening happened for me. I had been in stillness, breathing deeply, asking for nothing. And suddenly, I was overcome by a flood of remembrance—not of facts or timelines, but of **essence**. I saw the patterns of creation. I felt the rhythm of the Universe within my own heartbeat. I knew I was not separate from anything I had been seeking. I *was* what I was searching for.

John's experience in the chamber of light mirrored my own. As he merged with the divine intelligence encoded within him, he stopped trying to become something and simply began *being it.* That is the great turning point: When the seeker becomes the source. When the initiate remembers he was never not divine.

You Are the Light You've Been Waiting For

Now you, dear reader, stand at the threshold of your own return.

This story was never meant to end with the final chapter. It is meant to begin again…in your life. In your choices. In your awakening. You are now the one standing before the pyramid, prepared to walk into its mystery. You are the one being asked to **trust the dark**, **find the center**, and **become the light**.

The transformational power of this journey is real. I have lived it. And as someone who walked through the fire, I am here to tell you: Something unspeakably beautiful is on the other side.

When you surrender to your Higher Self's guidance, you no longer live as a fragmented being pulled in a thousand directions. You begin to live in alignment. You speak with clarity. You create with power. You love with truth. You become a vessel for the core divine qualities that have always existed within you—peace, love, compassion, courage, wisdom, radiance.

And from that place, you no longer seek to change the world…. **You become the change**.

So I leave you with this invitation: Apply what you've learned. Not just in moments of crisis, but in every breath. Let the pyramid within you awaken. Let the chambers be entered again and again—each time with deeper reverence. Let your life be the altar where your soul speaks.

You are not broken. You are being reborn.

You are not lost. You are remembering.

You are not alone. You are now, and have always been, an initiate.

With love and deep gratitude for your courage to walk this path,

Ben Neil
Author of *The Initiate*
Fellow traveler on the sacred road home

ABOUT THE AUTHOR

Awakened. Visionary. Timeless.

Ben Neil is more than an author, he is a modern initiate, a guide, and a weaver of stories that awaken the soul. Through *The Initiate* series of books and courses, Ben opens ancient doors of remembrance, blending timeless wisdom with visionary storytelling that inspires readers to step into their own sacred journey of transformation.

His path did not begin in light, but in fire. In 2009, Ben entered the crucible of the Dark Night of the Soul—a complete unraveling of identity and belief. It was in that darkness that the seed of *The Initiate* was planted. What emerged was not simply fiction, but testimony: a living map born of experience, initiation, and awakening. The first novel, *The Initiate*, is a chronicle of that passage. Its sequel, *The Initiate: Remembering*, carries the journey forward, where the mirrors of relationship became teachers, revealing hidden soul memories and timeless truths.

For over two decades, Ben has immersed himself in the mysteries of consciousness, studying sacred geometry, metaphysics, Jungian psychology, esoteric traditions, energy medicine, and the wisdom of ancient mystery schools. Yet his true gift lies not only in knowledge but in presence. As an empath and visionary, Ben writes with a depth that touches readers at a cellular level, awakening what has always been within them.

At the heart of his work is a single belief: we are all Initiates. Beneath our pain, distractions, and forgotten stories lies a divine remembrance waiting to be reclaimed. Through layered symbolism, archetypal journeys, and immersive prose, Ben reminds every reader: **you are not broken, you are remembering.**

The Initiate series is more than storytelling—it is initiation. Whether through a novel, a course, or a single spoken word, Ben transmits a frequency of remembering that activates transformation and calls us home to ourselves. His mission is simple yet profound: to guide seekers, mystics, and wanderers into the sacred chambers of their own consciousness, where ancient memory whispers and true identity awakens.

Ben Neil's voice is visionary and intimate, mystical yet deeply human. His promise is to take readers beyond story—into soul. His invitation is clear: step into the remembrance of who you are. For your story has always been sacred, and your journey has always been initiation.

A Sneak Peek at *The Initiate Book 2: Remembering*

1

MICHAEL

I arrived early.

The café hadn't changed—the same quiet little nook remained nestled between two worn brick buildings, ivy creeping up their sides like nature reclaiming forgotten stone. It had always felt like neutral ground, a place where time softened around the edges. But today, the air felt different. Charged maybe. Or expectant.

Then I saw him.

John.

He walked toward me with a quiet confidence that stopped me cold. It had been months—months of unraveling for me—and yet here he was, not unraveled but somehow rewoven. His steps reflected a calm, a steady grace I hadn't seen before. His presence hit me like warmth after a long freeze. Gone was the haunted man who had left for Egypt, eyes shadowed and heart clenched. This John looked...free.

He smiled.

Not the strained, polite kind of smile we exchange with strangers, but a genuine, knowing one. The smile reached all the way into his eyes, and in that moment, I knew—something profound had shifted in him. His eyes held a depth, a stillness, like he'd been somewhere

ancient and come back with answers. Answers I desperately needed.

We sat, facing each other, the quiet hum of the café
blurring into the background. I studied him. An undeniable contrast existed between us. John looked like a man
who had found the sun after a lifetime in the shadows.
Me? I was barely holding it together.

I hadn't slept. My body throbbed with exhaustion, my
soul even more so. The weight of financial collapse was
crushing, but worse was the silence that had taken up
residence in my home. The silence left by Amber—my
wife. Her absence echoed through the walls like a scream
muffled by time. And I hated it. I hated the emptiness,
the questions, and the unbearable finality of it all.

John didn't press. He didn't need to. He looked at
me, and I knew he saw it all. The pain. The resentment.
The slow, venomous rage eating through me.

He didn't speak right away. I think he wanted to.
Maybe he didn't know how to reach me through all the
walls I'd built. Or maybe he knew the words weren't what
mattered. So I asked about Egypt—about what had happened there.

His eyes flickered—something ancient stirring just
below the surface. He spoke slowly, deliberately. He didn't
tell me everything, but what he did share painted images
I couldn't shake. Visions of a past life, of sacred places, of
transformation. And behind every word, I sensed a storm
of memories he wasn't ready to say aloud.

Then he mentioned a name.

William Allbright.

A pulse of recognition. The name rang through me
like a bell. I had followed William's work for years. He

was more than a hugely successful businessman—he was an icon, an innovator, a genius. And now John was telling me they'd become close?

I leaned forward, hungry for connection. For clarity. For hope. I asked—maybe too eagerly—if I could meet him.

John nodded.

And in that single gesture, something flickered back to life in me. A fragile spark in a long-cold hearth. Maybe this wasn't the end. Maybe it was the beginning of something I couldn't yet name.

Maybe John had found a path—and maybe, just maybe, he'd come back to show me the way.

2

JOHN

I stepped out of the coffee shop and into the crisp air, but the cold couldn't numb the heaviness in my chest. It wasn't just sadness—it was something deeper, something like grief mixed with helplessness. A quiet ache had settled into my bones, and I knew it wouldn't go away easily. Seeing Michael like that, unraveling under the weight of his own pain, pierced through me like a blade. He had always been the strong one, the grounded one. But now? He looked like a man being slowly consumed from the inside out.

Seeing him brought back everything I thought I'd finally put to rest—the accident, the loss of Sara and Christina, my wife and my daughter. Gone in an instant, torn from the world and from me. I remember that emptiness, the way grief hollowed me out until I felt like a ghost in my own skin. And through it all, Michael had been there. Steady. Loyal. He showed up when I couldn't speak, when the only sound I could make was silence. He held space for me when I didn't even know I needed it.

And now he was walking through his own fire.

His eyes told the story his mouth wouldn't. Disillusionment. Fatigue. That flickering desperation of someone who no longer believes the sun will rise again.

He was slipping into that space between numbness and despair—the place where hope feels like a foreign language. I knew it well. William knew it too. And so I told myself, "Even if I can't fix it, even if I can't say the perfect words to bring him back, I will not abandon him."

I wanted to tell him everything. I wanted to share the truth of what I had experienced in Egypt—the ancient visions, reconnecting with Sara, the sacred revelations, the miracle of memory returning from a past lifetime. I wanted him to know the magic I had touched, the divine presence that had shown me a world beyond logic. But Michael doesn't live in that world. He clings to reason like a life raft, his mind armored against anything that can't be quantified. The mystical doesn't fit into the framework he's built to protect himself from more heartbreak.

And still...I have hope.

Because if anyone can reach him, it's William Allbright.

Michael had revered William for years. Not just as a business icon, a self-made billionaire with global influence, but as a man. As a soul. Michael saw in William what he wished he could become—confident, successful, grounded. He didn't know that William carried his own scars, his own shadowed past. He, too, had been broken. He, too, had lost everything when his wife and son died in that tragic plane crash. The difference? William found a way to turn his suffering into wisdom.

When the Universe brought William into my life, I knew it wasn't by accident. And now, that same mysterious current was guiding him to Michael. I felt it—this deep, unshakable knowing that something powerful was in motion.

As I drove to the airport to meet William, that feeling grew. The air itself felt charged with purpose. The roads stretched before me like a path carved by something ancient and wise. I could almost hear the whispers of destiny riding the wind.

This wasn't a coincidence. This was grace.

The same invisible hand that had carried me through my grief was reaching out now for Michael. I saw him in my mind, sitting alone in that echoing house, haunted by silence and the ghosts of what once was. I remembered what that felt like. To be broken. To believe joy would never return.

And I remembered the moment he reached for me, without expectation, without judgment. Just love.

Now it was my turn.

With William by my side, I would step into that darkness. I would find the place where Michael had gone to hide. And together, we would remind him of who he truly was.

Maybe, just maybe, Michael's awakening was why we had all come together.

Maybe the Universe had been preparing us for this moment all along.

3

JOHN

The call came just hours before Michael and William were meant to meet.

A motorcycle accident. Michael was in critical condition. Coma.

The words didn't land all at once. They felt distant, like an echo through thick fog. My breath caught in my throat. The walls around me seemed to close in, warping with the weight of disbelief. I had just seen Michael. I had just felt the first flicker of light return to his eyes. And now this?

I clutched the phone tighter, as if my grip could somehow twist time, rewind the moment, undo what had just unfolded. My knuckles turned white.

William was already with me when the call came in. I saw his expression shift as I relayed the news—no questions, no hesitation. Just silent, immediate understanding. We were out the door before the dial tone faded.

The hospital was sterile and cold, too white, too clean. The kind of place where everything felt suspended in some artificial stillness. We were led through winding halls that all looked the same until, finally, we stepped into Michael's room.

Machines beeped softly, rhythmically. Oxygen hissed. The air was thick with the scent of antiseptic and quiet despair. My eyes landed on him—my best friend, broken and motionless in the bed. Tubes wove in and out of his body like veins from another world. Bruises marred his skin. A bandage wrapped around his head. His face, though pale, still held the same shape I'd known since we were boys.

But it wasn't just the sight of him that undid me. It was the weight of what he had been to me. Michael had held me up when I collapsed. After the accident that took Sara and Christina, he became my lifeline. He didn't try to fix me—he just stayed. He reminded me what it meant to keep breathing. And now, it was his turn to be in the fire.

William stood still beside me. Silent. At first, I thought it was shock. But then I saw something in his face that shook me. Recognition. Deep, haunted recognition.

William's mouth opened, and the words came low, barely audible: "I know him."

I turned sharply. "What did you say?"

He blinked slowly, swallowing hard. "He feels...familiar. I—I don't know how to explain it."

I didn't press him. I saw the tremble in his hands, the tightening of his jaw. He was battling something unseen, something old. He sat down slowly in the chair by the bed, like the weight of the moment had suddenly become too much.

"Tell me about him," he said.

So I did. I told him about our childhood. About the way we grew up side by side, about the years and the fights and the laughter. I told him how Michael's life had unraveled lately—how the pressures of his business failures had crushed him. And then the final, cruel twist: his wife leaving him for another man, Eric Jones. The name tasted bitter even now.

As I finished, I saw William's face twist with a complex pain.

"My wife, Diana...she was having an affair with Earl Buckingham, my CFO," he said, his voice brittle. "For years. Before she died."

Silence fell between us, but it wasn't empty. It was charged. Something unseen rippled beneath it—a thread, invisible and ancient, connecting these losses, these betrayals. It wasn't just a coincidence. It couldn't be.

William pressed his palms to his eyes, trying to hold himself together. I could feel the storm in him, the way it mirrored my own.

Then the doctor came in.

He was kind. Calm. He explained the injuries—traumatic brain damage, internal bleeding, and swelling. They had done what they could. Stabilized Michael. But his condition was still critical.

"What he needs now," the doctor said, "is time. His body has done all it can. The rest...is up to something greater."

William stood and stepped forward. "Anything he needs," he said firmly, "whatever it costs, just make sure he has what he needs to heal."

The doctor nodded, grateful but cautious. He left us alone again.

We stayed there for hours. Not saying much. Just watching. William never took his eyes off Michael.

I finally reached out, placing my hand gently on Michael's arm. His skin was warm. Alive.

"Come back, Brother," I whispered. "You're not done. There's more for you here. So much more."

And in that stillness, I felt something shift. It wasn't loud. It wasn't obvious. But it was there—a faint pulse, a thread of energy that shimmered in the space between us. He was still here.

And I wasn't letting go.

4

JOHN

I returned to the hospital every day.

Sometimes I brought books—old favorites of Michael's, stories we had once shared—and read aloud in soft, steady tones. Other times, I simply sat beside him, allowing the silence to stretch between us while the machines around us clicked and sighed, keeping time in the language of blinking lights and beeping rhythms. I'd watch the slight rise and fall of his chest, willing each breath to be a little stronger than the last. In those quiet hours, I wasn't sure who I was trying to comfort more—Michael or myself.

Visiting became a ritual. One I needed as much as I believed he did. A lifeline tethering me to the hope that somewhere, beyond the barrier of coma and trauma, Michael could still hear me. Still feel me. Still know he wasn't alone.

William came often. Most days, actually. He rarely spoke much, but his presence filled the room with a kind of still strength. We didn't need to talk. Something unspoken hung between us—an invisible tether of shared experience, shared heartbreak. We were two men drawn together by a mystery that neither of us could name, only feel. Something cosmic. Sacred.

One morning, I walked into the room to find William already there, seated in the same chair I always used. He was hunched forward, a worn leather notebook balanced on his knee, pen hanging from his fingers. His eyes weren't on the page. They were on Michael—distant, glassy, as if peering not at the man lying still in front of him, but through time itself.

I didn't speak. I just moved quietly to sit across from William and waited. The sunlight filtering through the blinds cast soft amber stripes across the sheets, gilding Michael's face in light that seemed too gentle for a place like this.

William finally stirred. He didn't look at me right away. His voice, when it came, was low and fragile.

"Michael saved me," he said. "In Peru."

My breath caught, just slightly. I felt the earth shift beneath us.

William turned his head slowly, his expression raw, vulnerable in a way I hadn't seen before. "I didn't remember it clearly until last night. It came back to me in a dream—or maybe it wasn't a dream. But it was him. It was Michael."

I wanted to ask him how he could be sure, but the words never made it out. I already knew. Deep down, I'd known all along.

"I was trapped," William went on. "In a place that felt ancient and terrible. I thought I was going to die there. And then Michael was just...there. As if he'd been waiting. Or called. He pulled me out. Not just from the place—but from something darker inside me."

The room seemed to still around us. The low hum of machines faded into the background, and all that remained was the truth stretching between us like a bridge made of memory.

"And when I woke up," he said, voice trembling, "I couldn't stop thinking about him. About this man I'd never met. Until I saw him. Here. In this bed."

I looked at Michael—his body unmoving, face serene, as though he were somewhere far away, dreaming of a place beyond our reach. And yet, he was here. With us. I felt it in the deepest part of me.

"He brought something back," I murmured, more to myself than to William. "Something more than memories."

William nodded. His eyes were shining now. "Maybe it's not just him. Maybe it's us too. Maybe we're all being called to remember."

The sun climbed higher outside, and its light spilled across Michael's blanket like a blessing. A warmth in a place defined by cold sterility. We sat together in that quiet reverence, not as men broken by life, but as souls slowly remembering something larger than themselves.

This was no ordinary accident.

And Michael was no ordinary man.